ROLF HEIMANN'S

BRAIN BUSTING BONANZA

LITTLE HARE

Little Hare Books
4/21 Mary Street, Surry Hills
NSW 2010 AUSTRALIA
www.littleharebooks.com

First published in 2003
Reprinted in 2005

National Library of Australia
Cataloguing-in-Publication entry

Heimann, Rolf, 1940-.
Rolf Heimann's brain-busting bonanza.

For children.
ISBN 1 877003 21 2.

1. Maze puzzles — Juvenile literature. I. Title.
793.738

Designed by ANTART
Printed in China
Produced by Phoenix Offset

5 4 3 2

Welcome to my biggest book ever of all-new mazes, puzzles,
spottos, conundrums, quizzes, teasers, stumpers and bafflers!

I was seven years old the first time I got lost in a maze.
It was a real maze, made from hedges.

Every turn I took either led to a dead end or to another fork.
I feared that I was stuck there forever, and I wondered how long
it would be before I starved to death. Then I suddenly found myself
at the exit—and this wonderful moment made it all worthwhile.

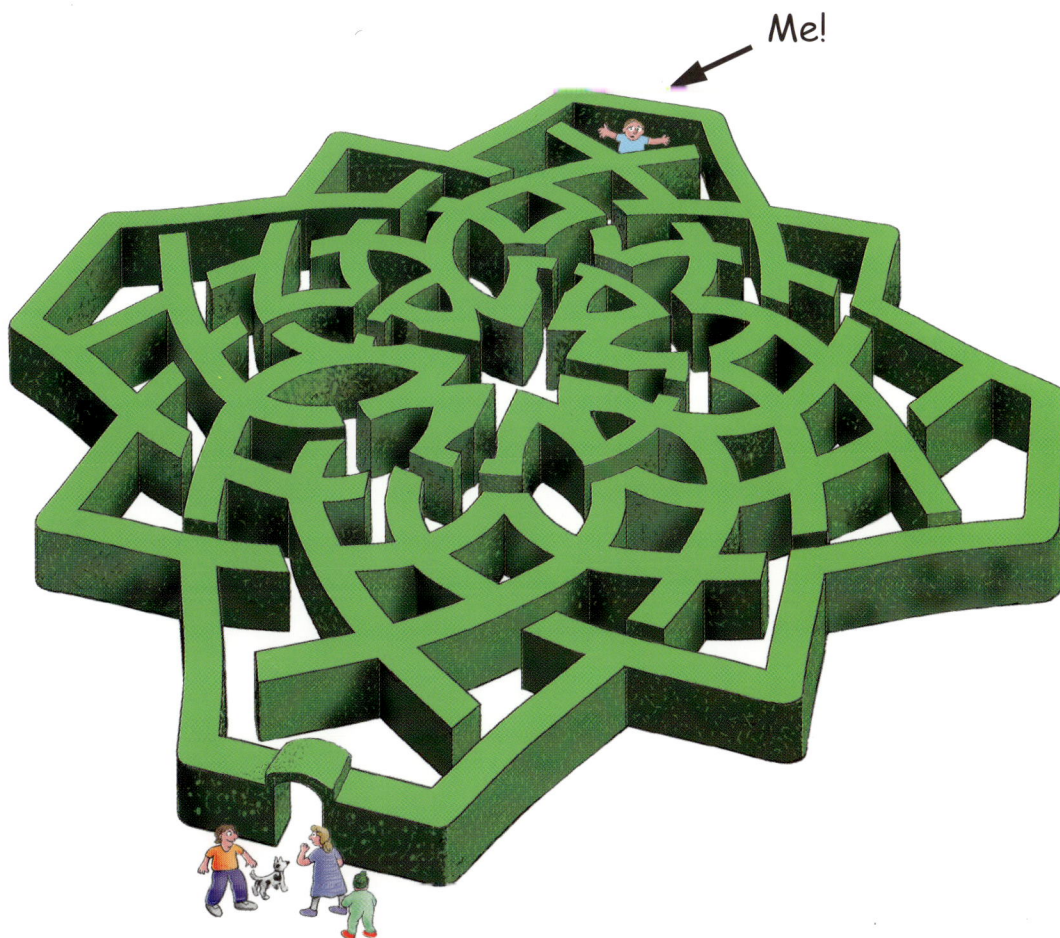

Me!

The moment of discovery—when you find your way out of a maze,
find a solution to a tricky puzzle, or work out the answer to a baffling
brain-buster—is the reason why people all over the world enjoy doing
puzzles and mazes. And one thing is for sure: nobody has ever starved
to death in any of *my* mazes!

(But you might starve if you try to do all the puzzles
and mazes in this bumper book without a break!)

 =  These equations show you the value of Schnoponian fruit.  =

1. Gift-giving In the galaxy of Schnopos III, it is very important that diplomats give each other gifts of equal value. Are the gifts being offered here equal?

2. Fruit platter Arrange these platters in order of their value.

1.

2.

3.

4.

5.

6.

3. Lost sock One of the diplomats has lost a tentacle sock. Which model does he have to buy?

4. Star-crossed snake
Help the snake find its way
to the nest below.

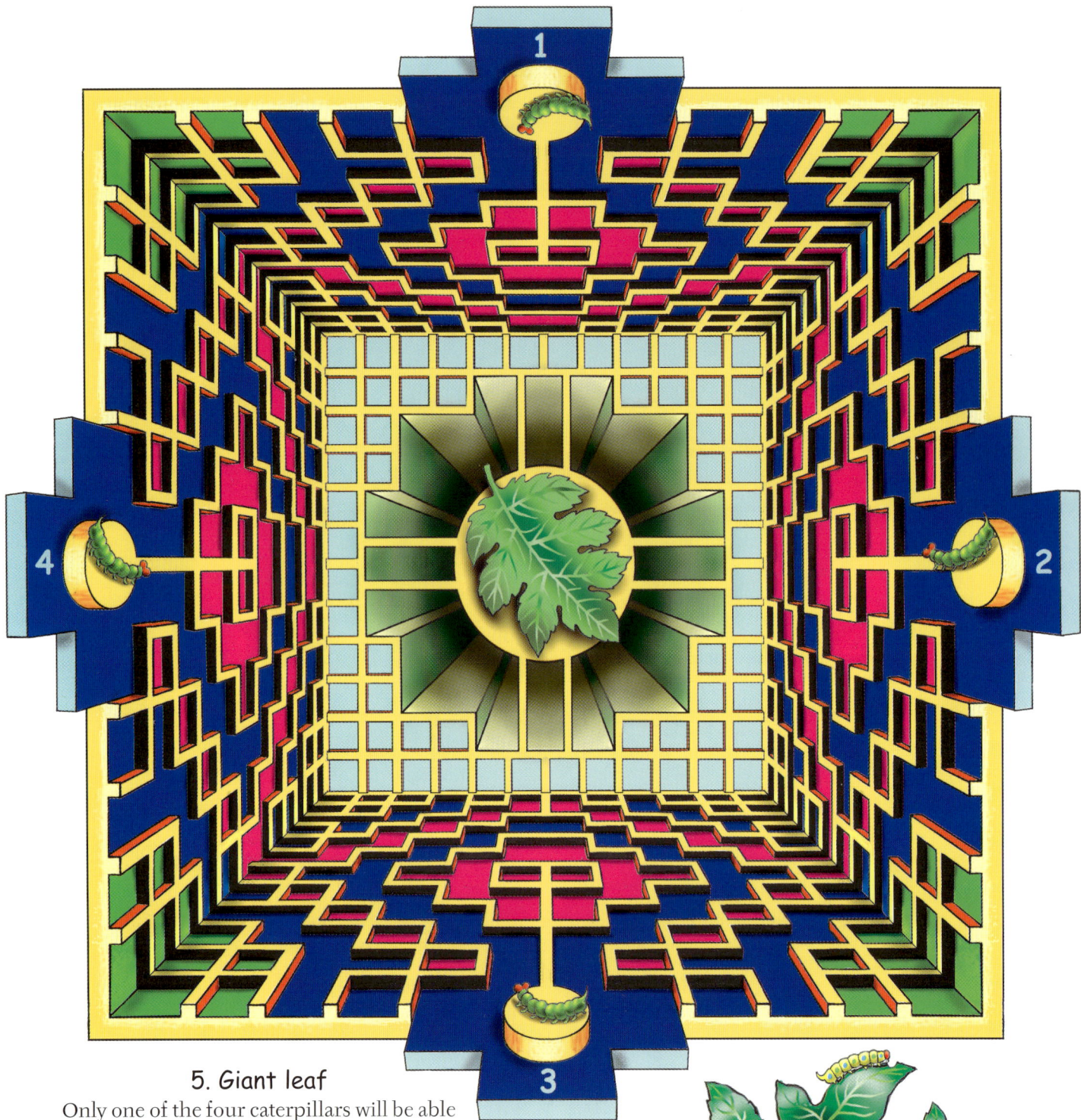

5. Giant leaf

Only one of the four caterpillars will be able
to reach the giant leaf. Which one?
(They can only walk on the yellow paths.)

6. Pillars of society

These caterpillars only like the company of
their own kind. Which one of them
doesn't belong?

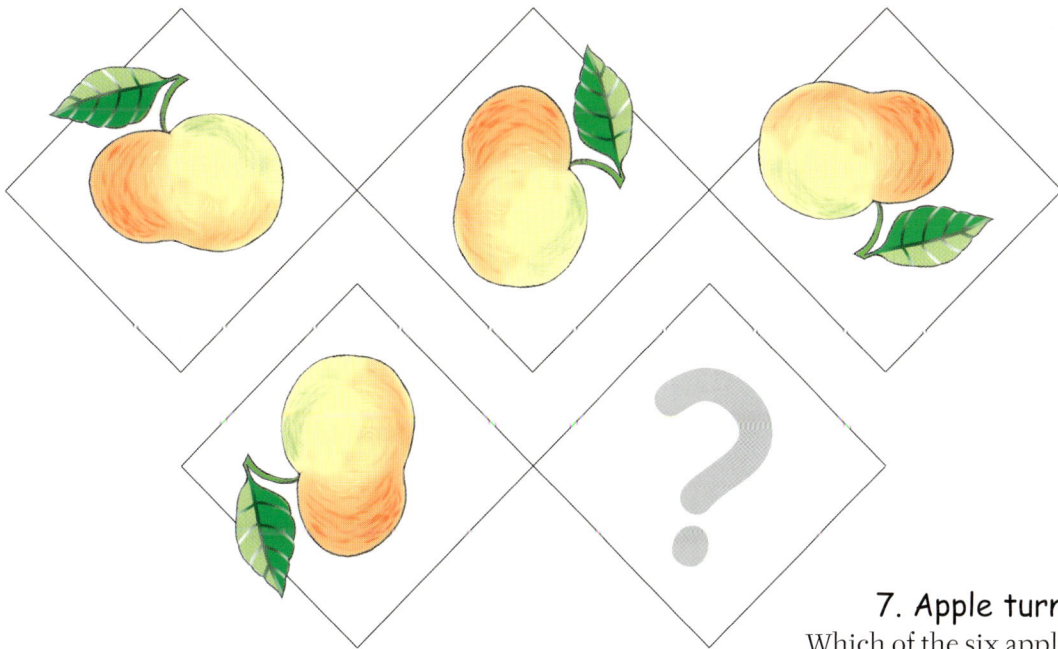

7. Apple turn-over
Which of the six apples below will fit into the empty square?

8. Brush-rush
Help the brush reach the paint pot.

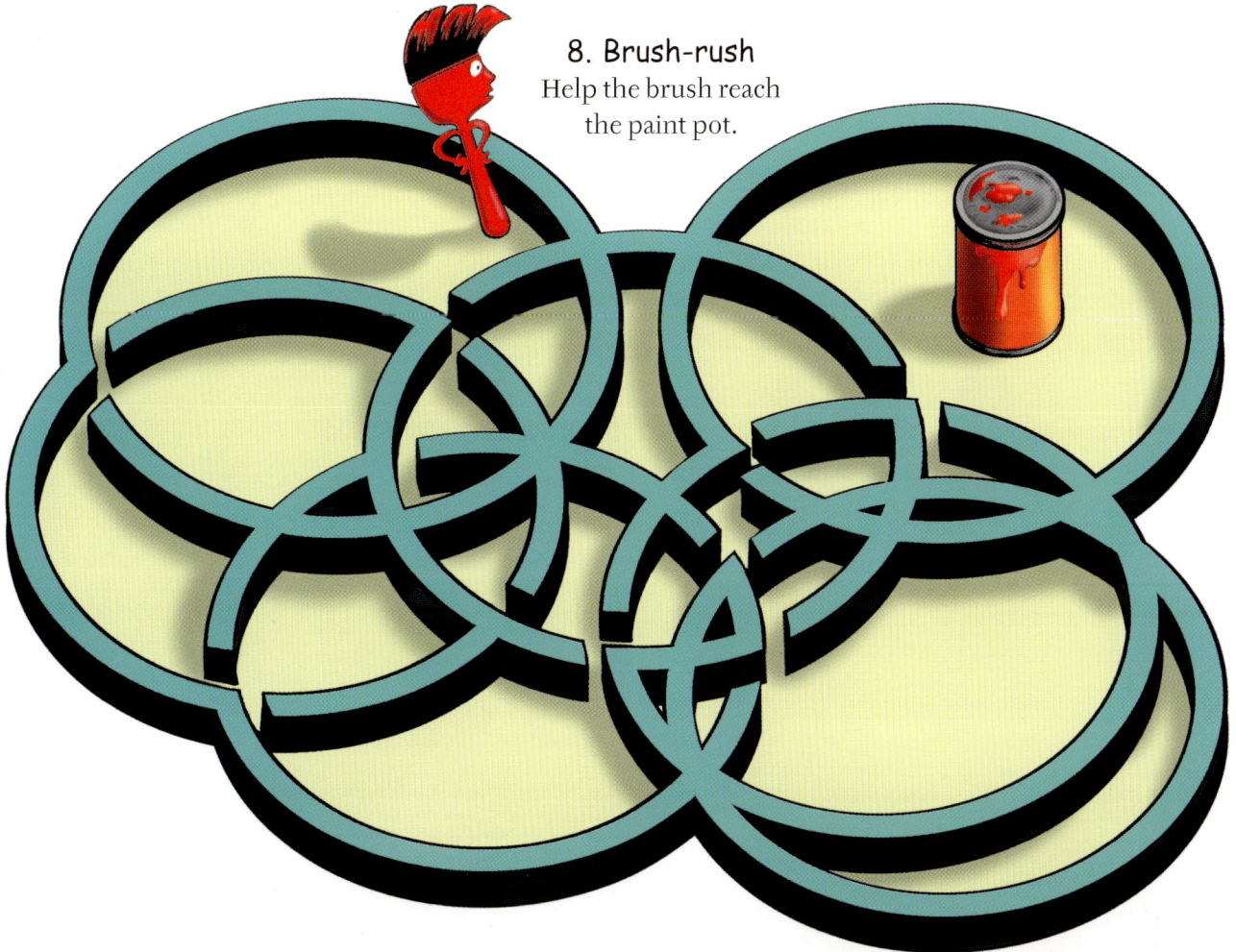

9. Double dragon trouble
Don't trust this reflection—no less than 25 spots are falsely mirrored!

10. Snail race

- Blue snails are twice as slow as yellow snails.
- Purple snails are three times faster than red snails.
- Red snails are twice as fast as blue snails.

Which of the four diagrams below shows their correct positions during the race?

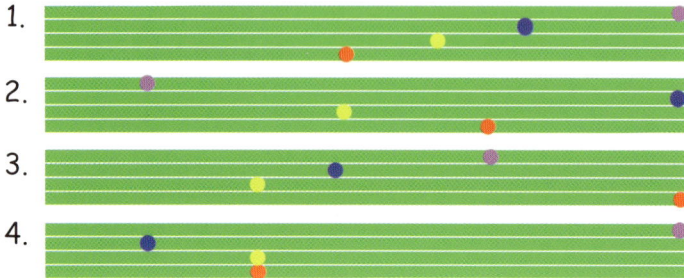

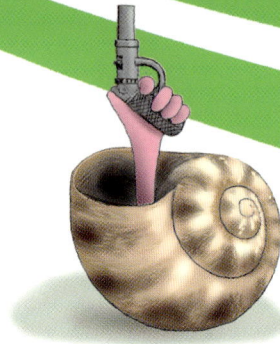

1.
2.
3.
4.

11. Family reunion

The Swirl family is having a reunion. The family members are of all ages and sizes, but one is definitely an outsider.

Which one and why?

12. Three-in-a-row
Find three-in-a-row of the following things:

Fish
Insects
Things with stripes
Things with dots

There is one picture left over. Which one?

13. Odd one out
Who or what is the odd one out?

14. Copied keys
Copies have been made of five of the six coloured keys— which one was forgotten?

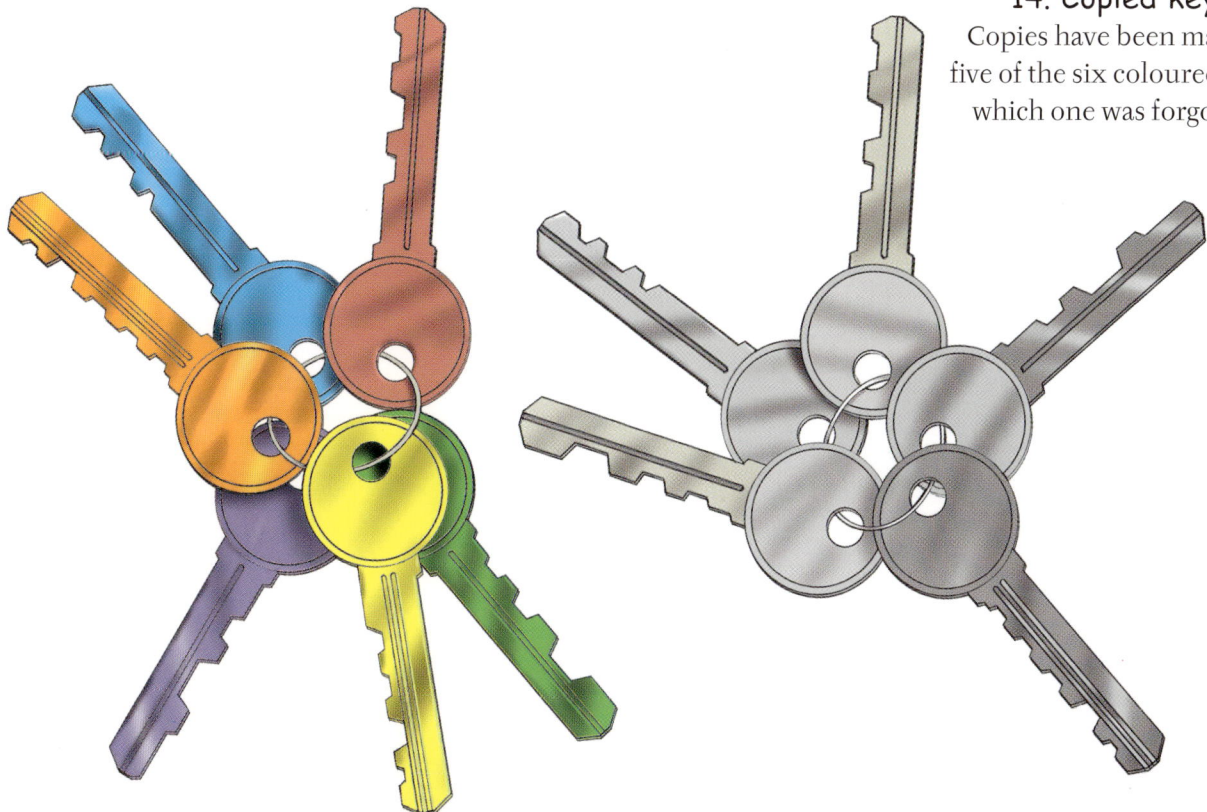

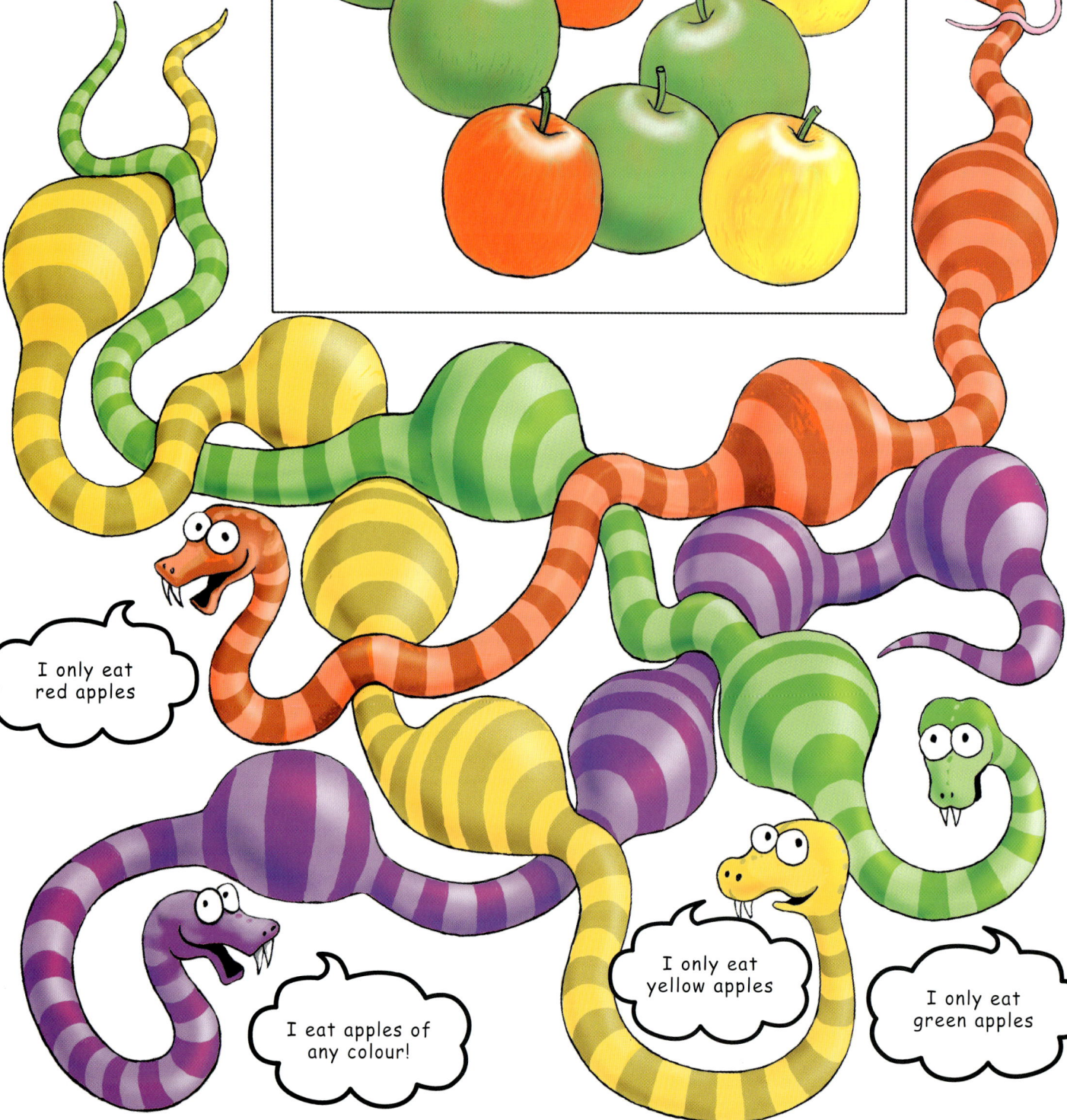

15. Apple snakes

Before the snakes got their hands on them, there were four green, four yellow and four red apples. What colour are the apples inside the purple snake?

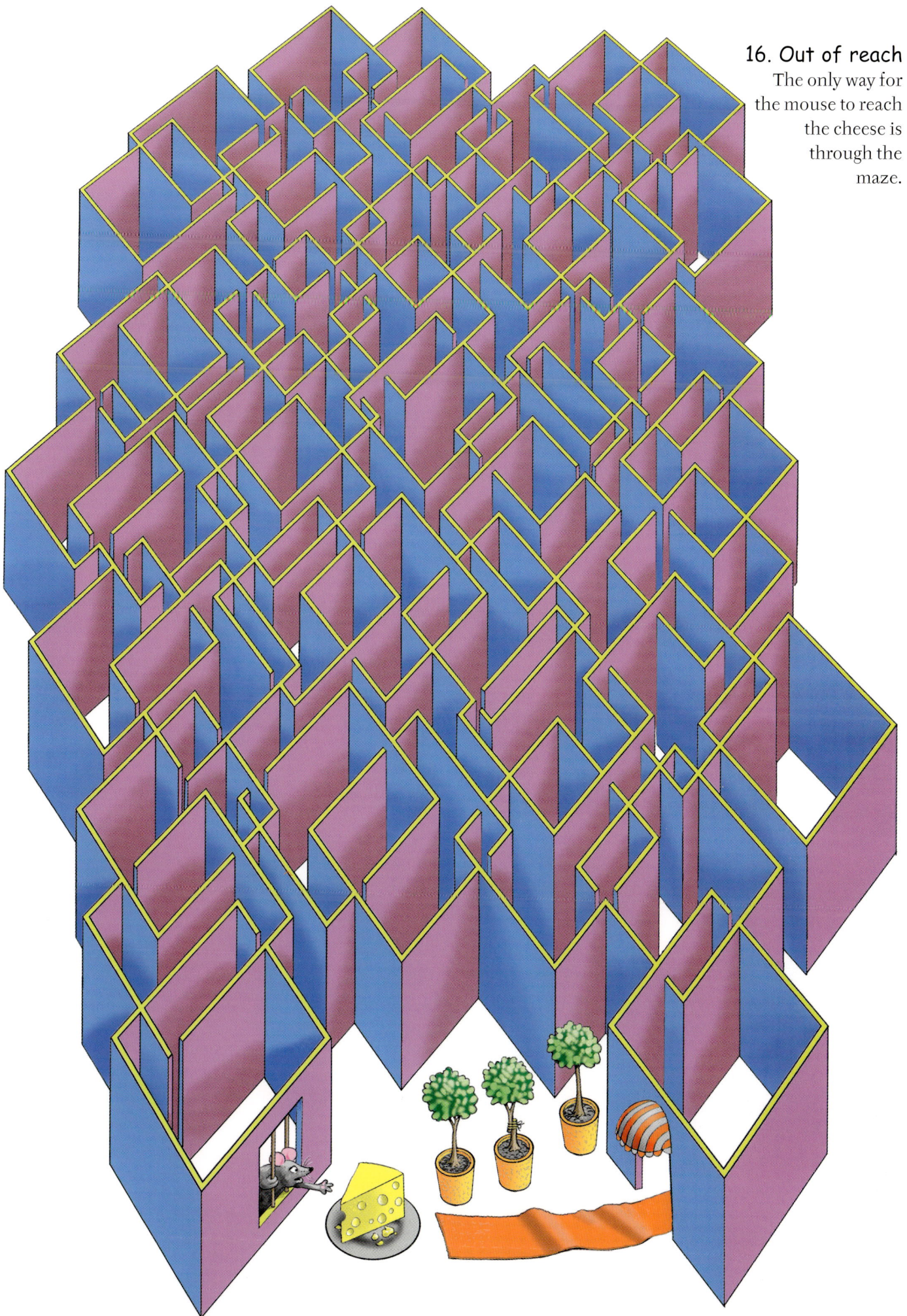

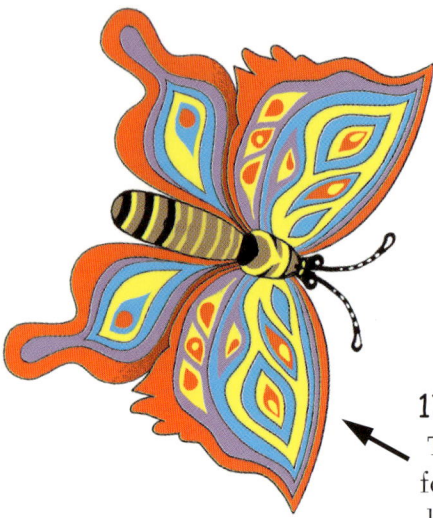

17. Butterfly friends

This butterfly is looking for a friend that is exactly like itself in every detail.

Which one could it be?

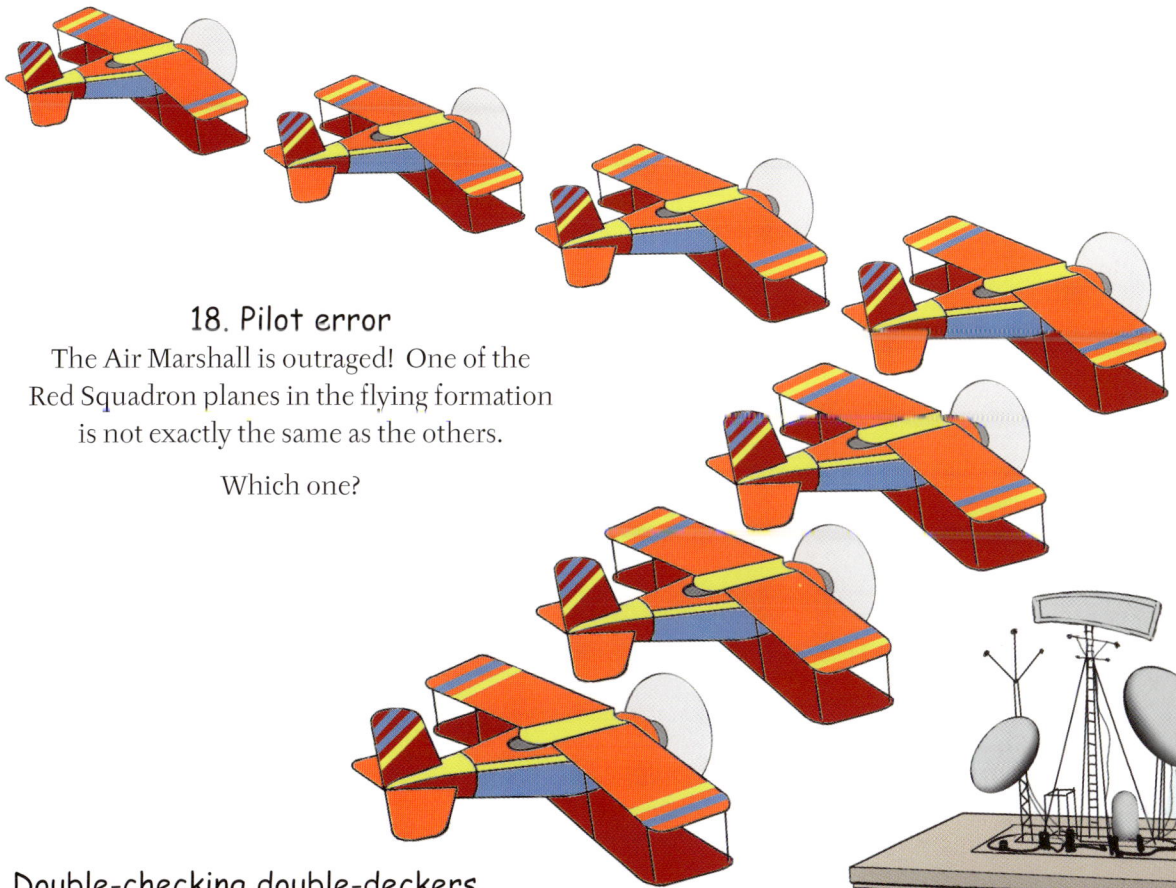

18. Pilot error

The Air Marshall is outraged! One of the
Red Squadron planes in the flying formation
is not exactly the same as the others.

Which one?

19. Double-checking double-deckers

When the pilots of the Yellow Squadron hear that
the Air Marshall is in a bad mood, they quickly check
their own planes. Uh oh!

Which one doesn't match...?

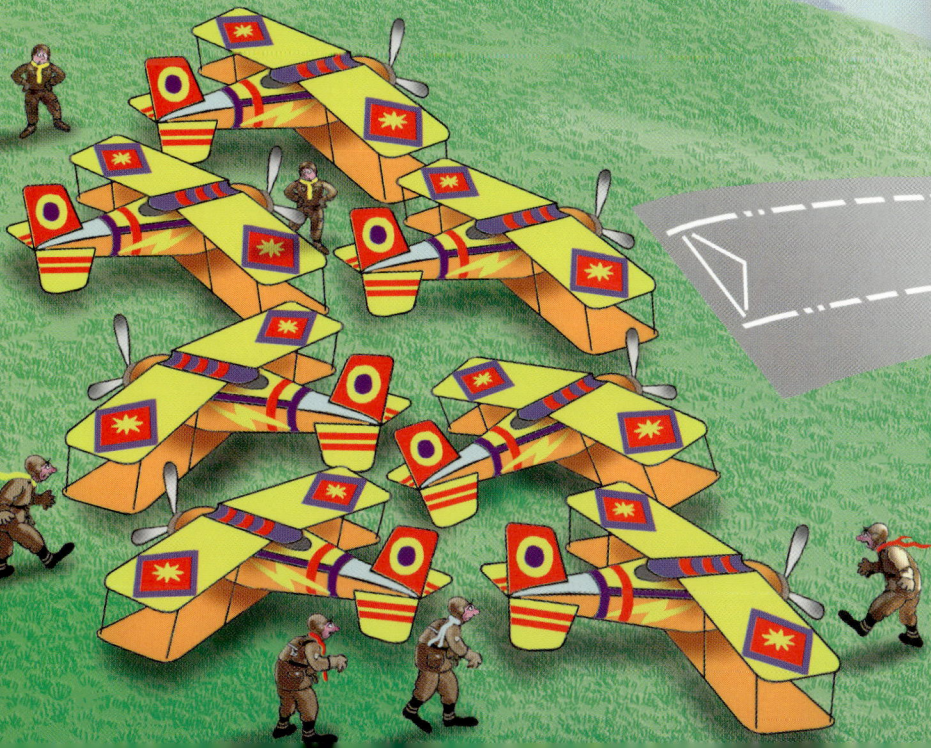

20. Day-dreamers

Have you ever noticed that sometimes clouds look like animals?

Spot at least a dozen here!

21. Fantastic faces

Trees—and even houses—often look like they have faces.

How many faces can you spot among these trees and houses?

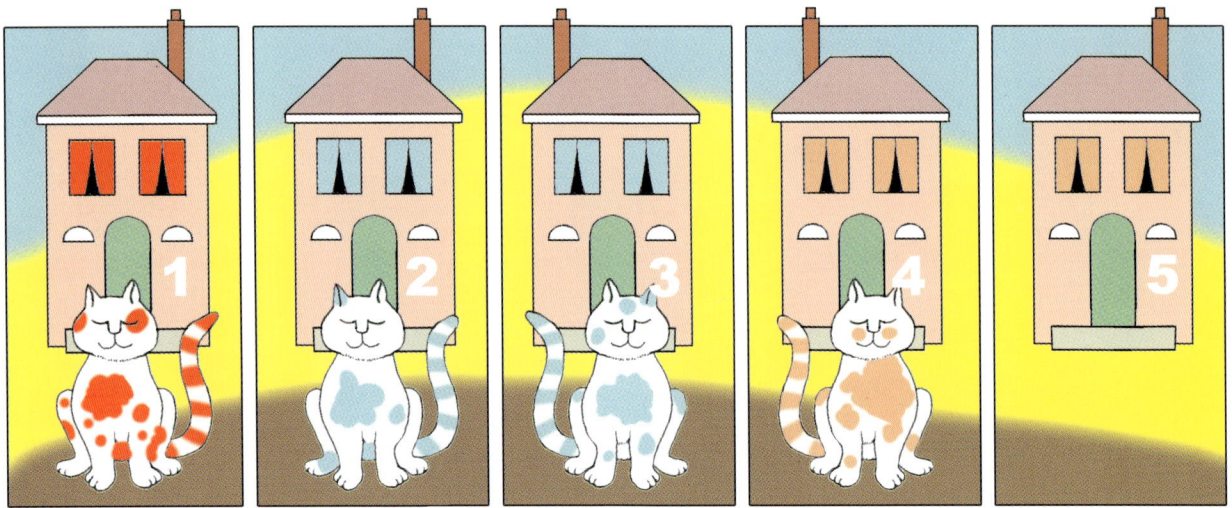

22. House cat Which one of the cats below lives at number 5?

23. Cat and mouse
How did the mouse escape through the maze?

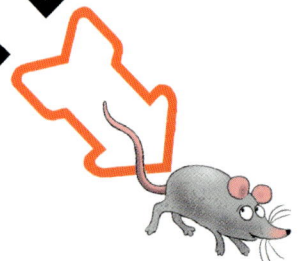

24. Special delivery
The brown parcel has to be delivered to a yellow house with a red roof and four chimneys.

Which number is the house?

25. Flower arrangement
The flowerbox is for the house that already has an identical arrangement.

Which house does it belong to?

26. Cat city!
How many cats are there?

Here's a hint: double the number of houses, then subtract the number of dogs you see.

27. Golden delicious

Why settle for little green apples when there's a ripe red one waiting?

Try to reach it without stepping over any lines.

28. Fractured star
Which one of the shapes below will complete the star?

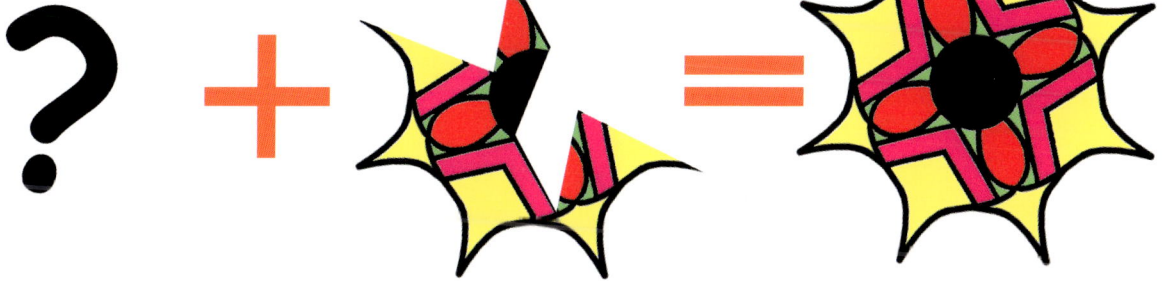

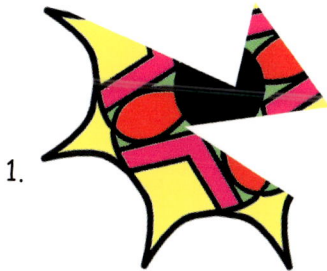

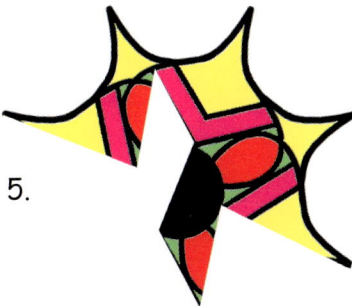

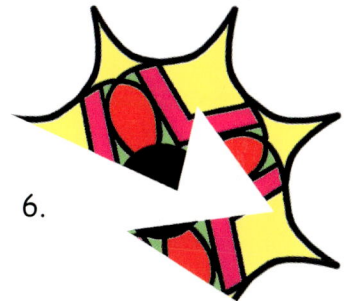

? + =

1.

2.

3.

4.

5.

6.

29. Missing mandolin
Which of the four pictures on the right belongs in the blank space?

1.

2.

3.

4.

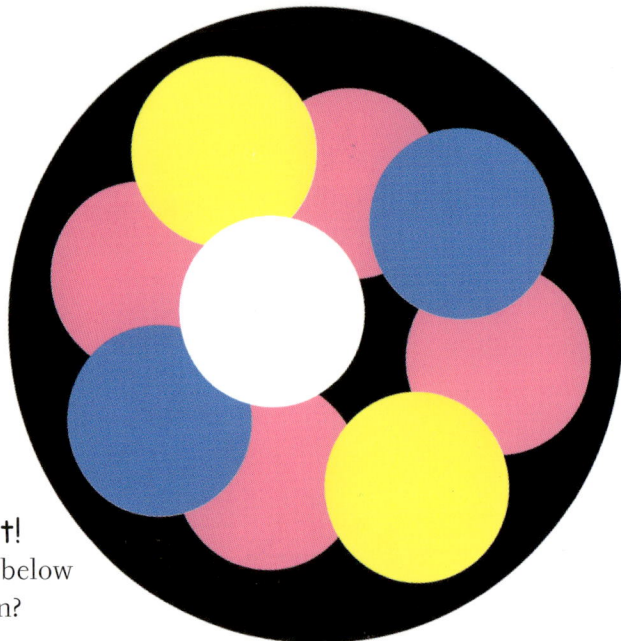

30. Missed a spot!
Which one of the circles below
is the missing section?

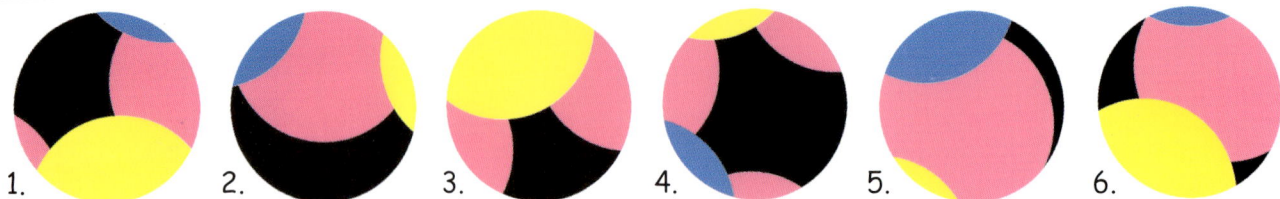

1.
2.
3.
4.
5.
6.

31. Through the butterfly
Go in one antenna and out the other!

32. Apple-loving grub

Help the grub find
its way to the apple.

33. Tree of life

If you think that the tree in the centre is symmetrical,
you're mistaken! Find three spots where it isn't...

34. Starry, starry jungle

Find your way from left to right.

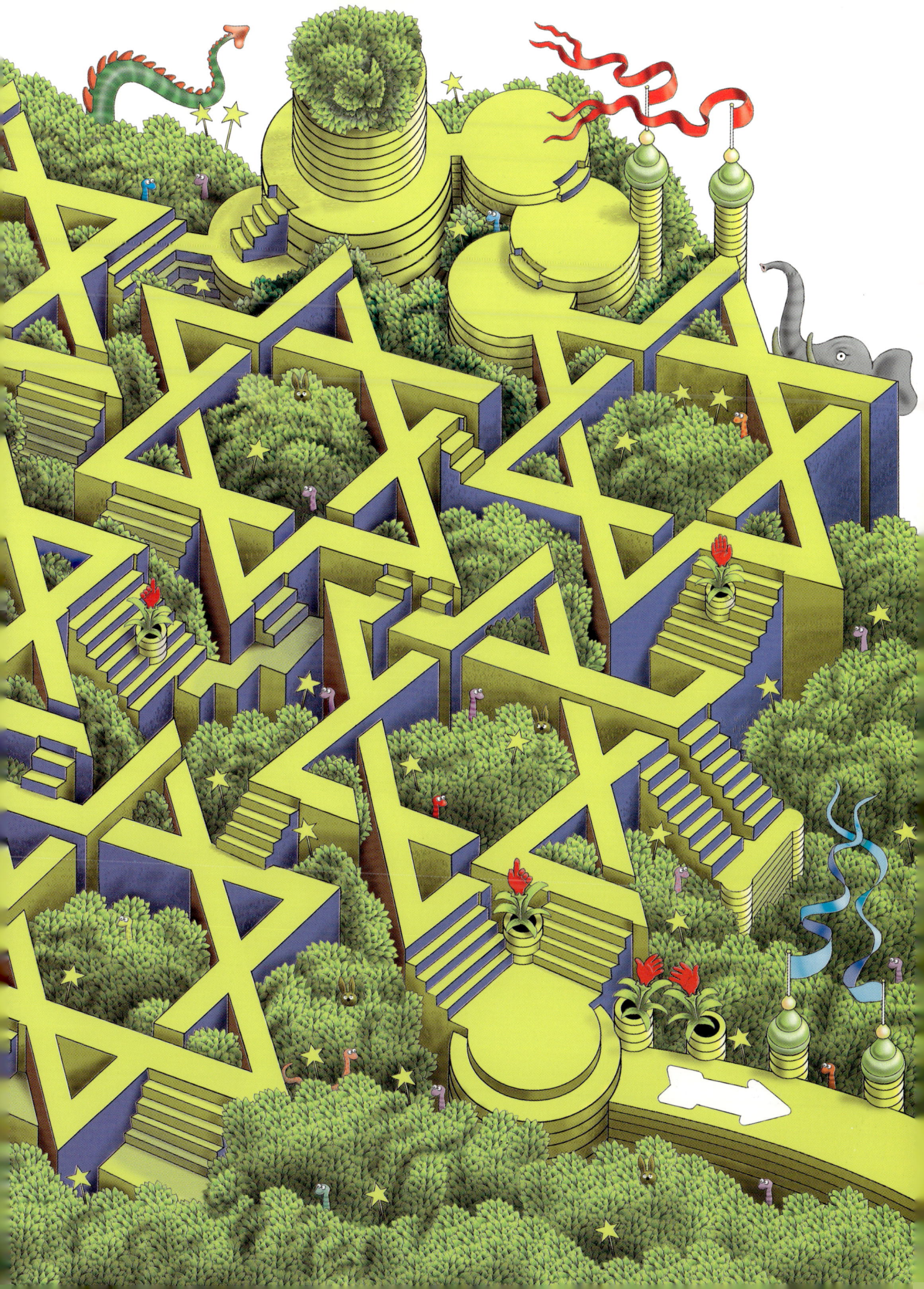

35. Magic mandala
Find your way out from the centre,
travelling only on the white lines.

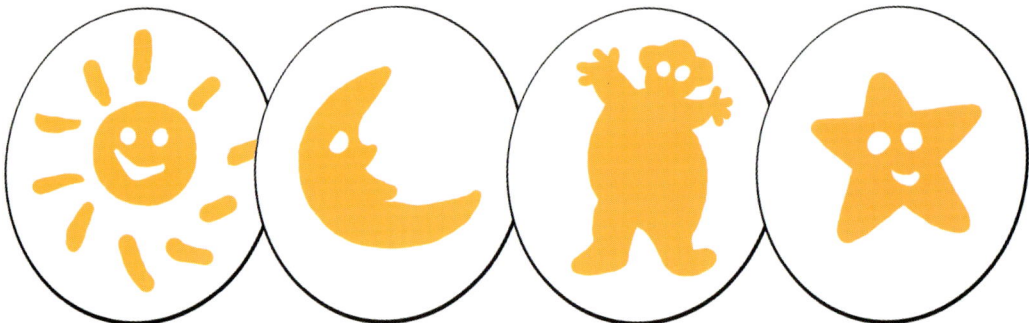

36. Odd one out Which of the pictures above doesn't belong?

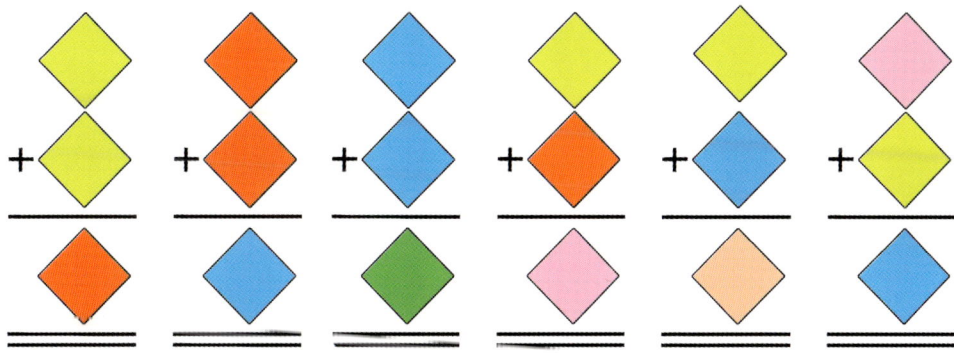

37. Colour code Work out what number each colour represents.

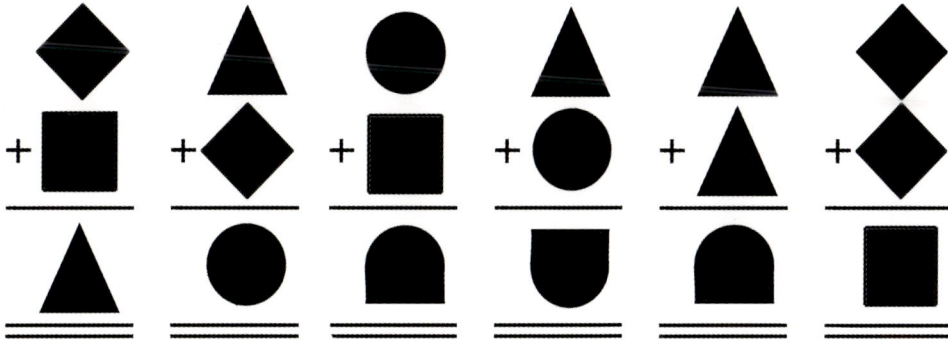

38. Shady deals In this puzzle, each shape represents a number.

39. Odd objects Each object stands for a number.

40. All together now Using the values above, you'll see that the items in the little box add up to three. But what do the items in the big box add up to?

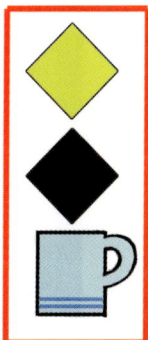

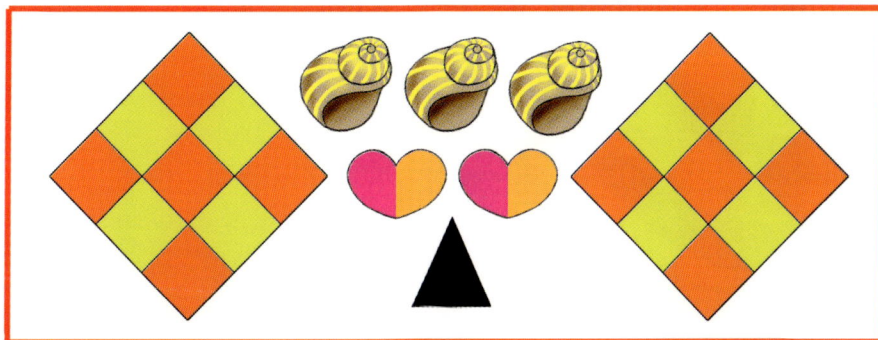

41. Odd one out

One of the items on the left doesn't belong.

Which one?

42. Vanishing violin case

Help the musician reach her violin case.

43. Notable error

In the notation of music, each note has a certain value (as shown here), and each bar must contain the same total.

full note	1/2	1/4	1/8	1/16

Check whether there is a mistake in one of the four bars below.

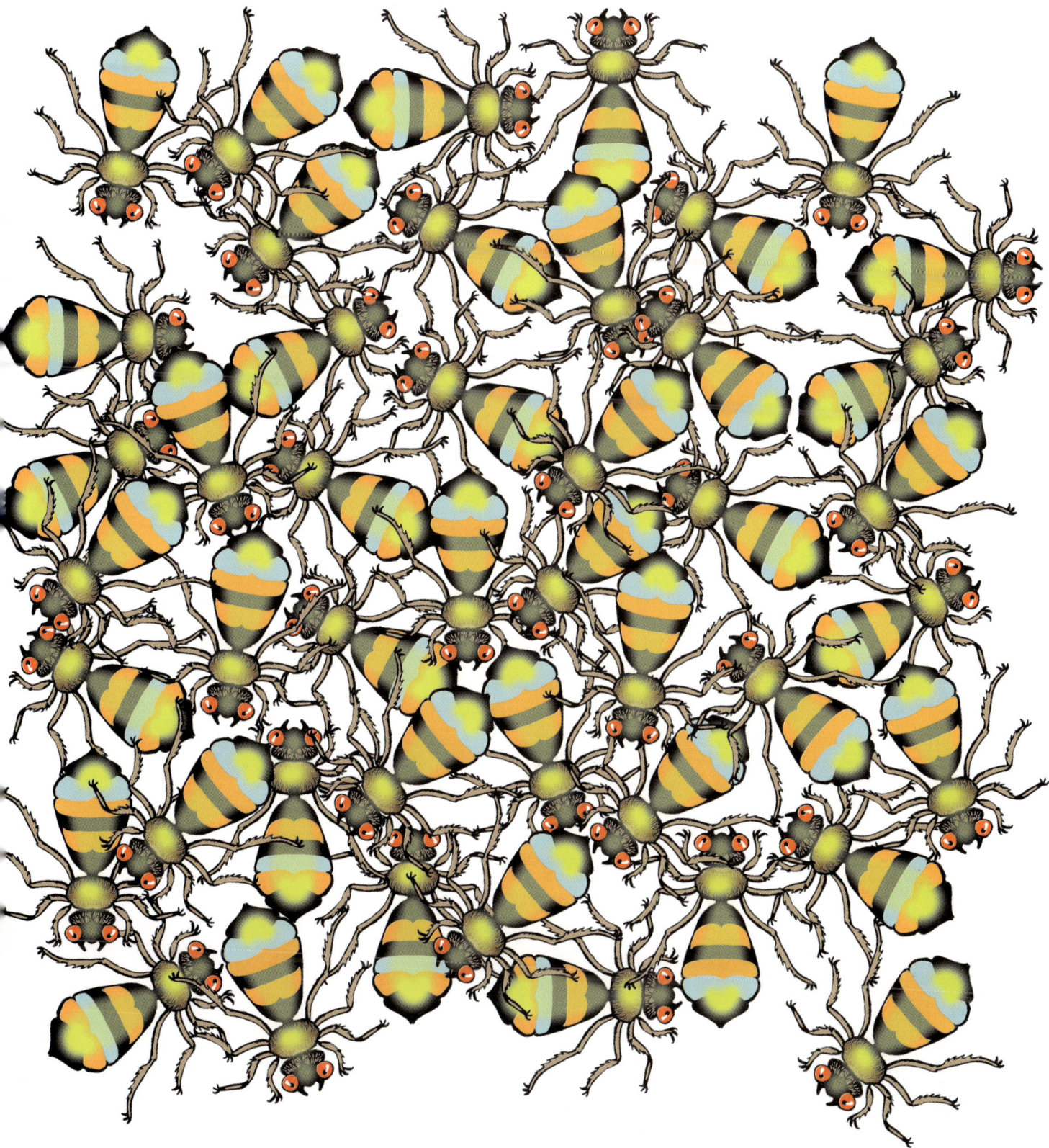

44. Spiders' nest

Scientists know that there are always more female honey spiders than male ones. Is the honey spider on the right male or female? (They're hard to tell apart, but they are definitely different.)

45. Coloured kites Which of the 12 pictures below fits into the blank space?
(Hint: look at the sequence of colours on the tail!)

46. Giddy geckos

Only three of the 64 geckos are able to reach the crown in the centre.

Which ones are they?

(Hint: It's the three geckos who look different to the others!)

47. Kite-flying competition

Only those who have dressed in the same colours as their kites are allowed to take part.

Are there are any children who should be disqualified?

48. Personal judgement

A special prize goes to the child who has dressed most like their kite.

(Warning: there's no correct answer. It's not easy being a judge, is it?!)

7kg

2.5kg

3kg

49. Super balloon

Red balloons can lift 7 kg.
Green ballons can lift 2.5 kg.
Blue balloons can lift 3 kg.

Which balloons will you
need to lift exactly 11 kg?

50. Lift-off!

What is the total weight
that this bunch of seven
balloons can lift?

11kg

51. Action Ant!

The ant in the middle needs to reach one of the leaves without stepping over any black lines.

If you're one of those smarties who begins a maze at the end and works back to the start, you'll be stumped here!

With these combinations of weight,
the see-saw is perfectly balanced.

52. Teetering tower
Find the correct counterweight.

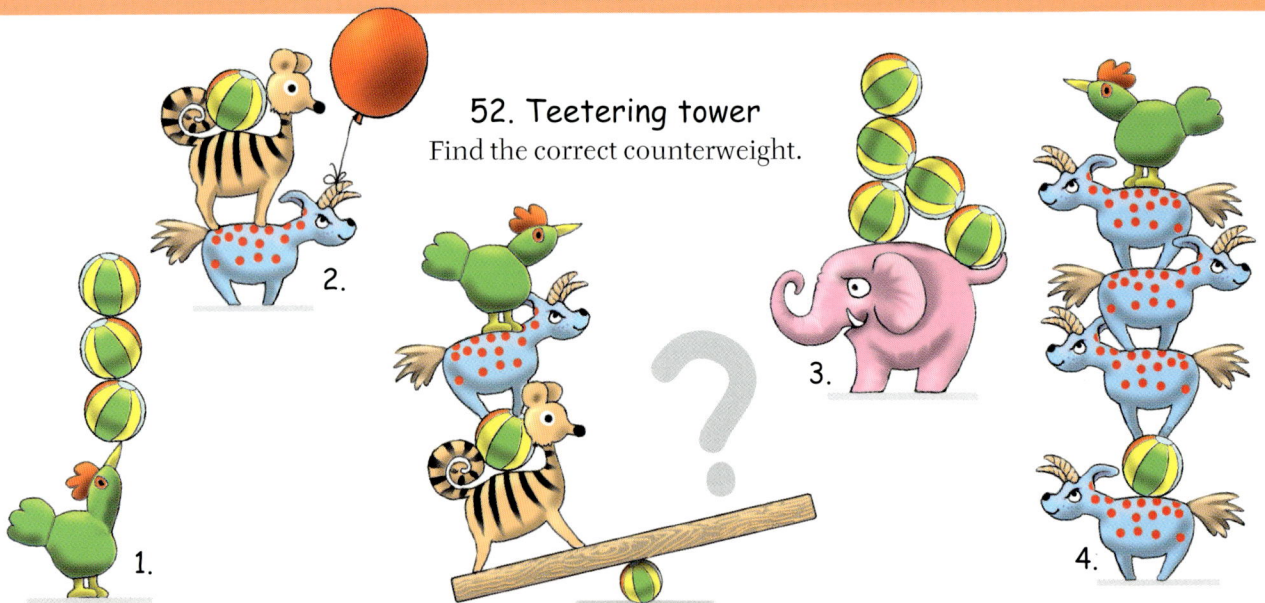

1.

2.

3.

4.

53. Shaky balance
Again, find the correct counterbalance.

1.

2.

3.

4.

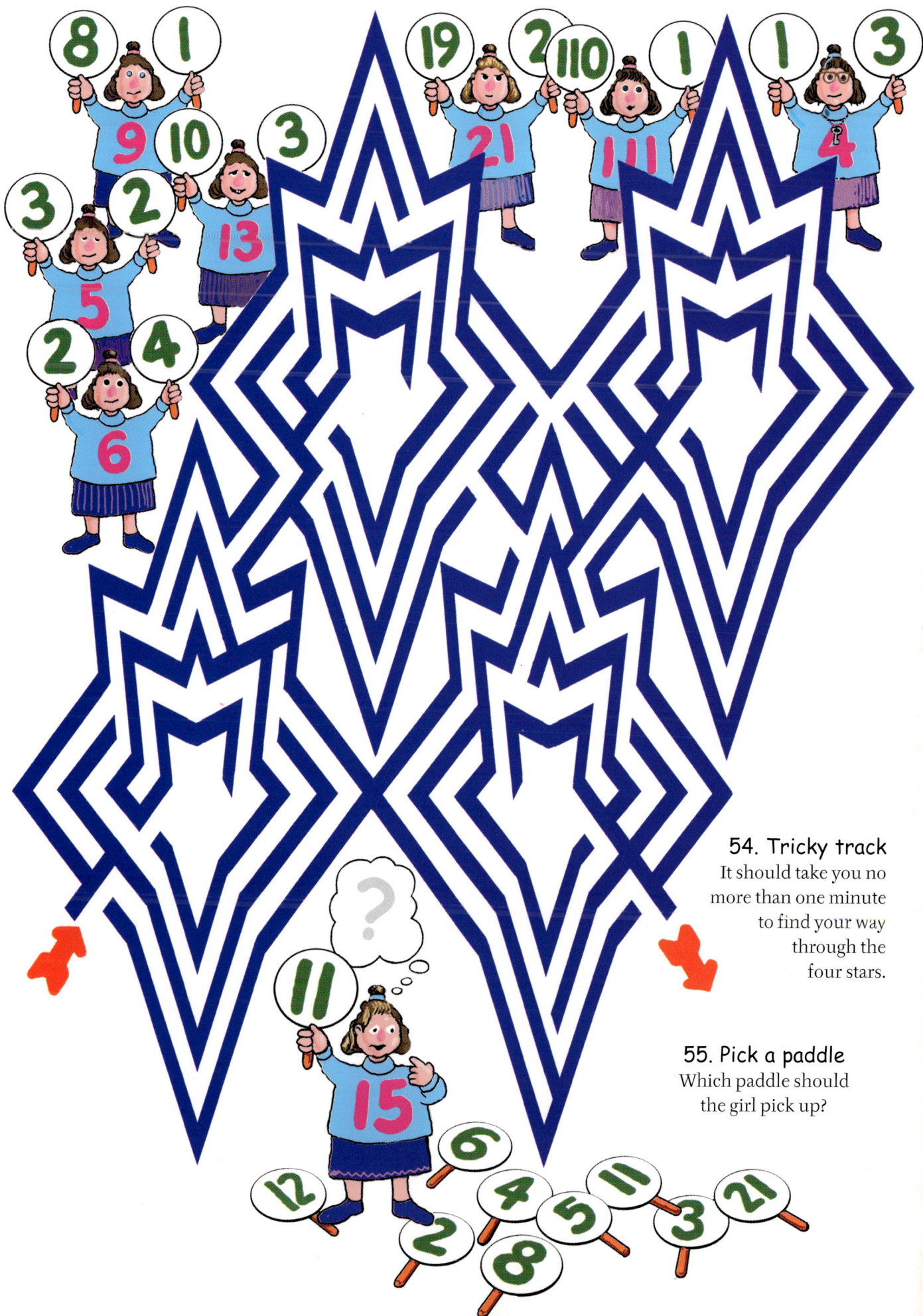

54. Tricky track
It should take you no more than one minute to find your way through the four stars.

55. Pick a paddle
Which paddle should the girl pick up?

56. Short delivery

Each door has been freshly painted in the colour of the house it belongs to.

But which one is missing?

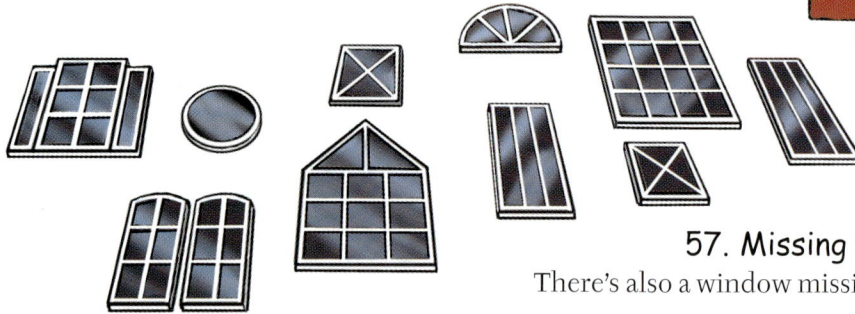

57. Missing window

There's also a window missing—for which house?

58. Trapped butterfly
For one of the butterflies, there is no escape!

59. Odd one out Which of the above objects is out of place?

60. Marsmathics Work out the value of the symbols.
The first picture will get you going!

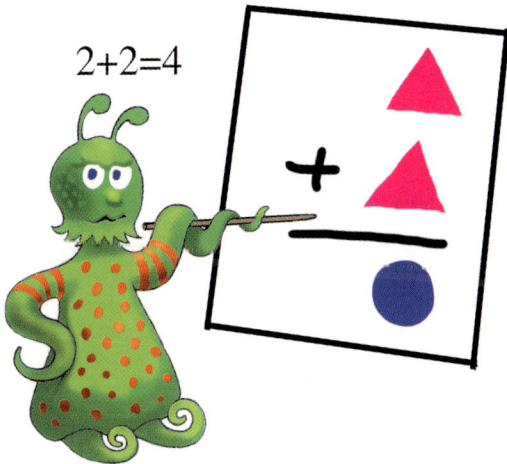

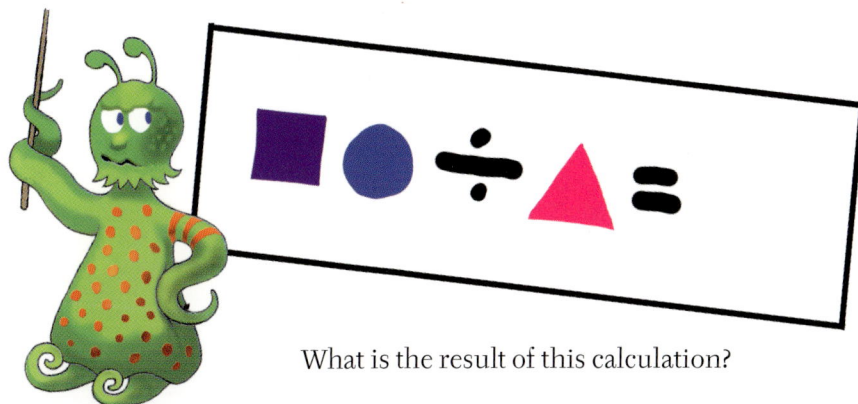

2+2=4

Translate this into Earth numbers!

What is the result of this calculation?

61. Galactic superstore

All the aliens agree that Joe has the best shop in the galaxy. Whatever you need, Joe is sure to have it.

But Joe doesn't speak all the alien languages, so they have to show him pictures of what they want.

Can Joe help his customers this time?

62. Ants' dilemma

Help the ants reach the sweets—but they must only walk on the black lines.

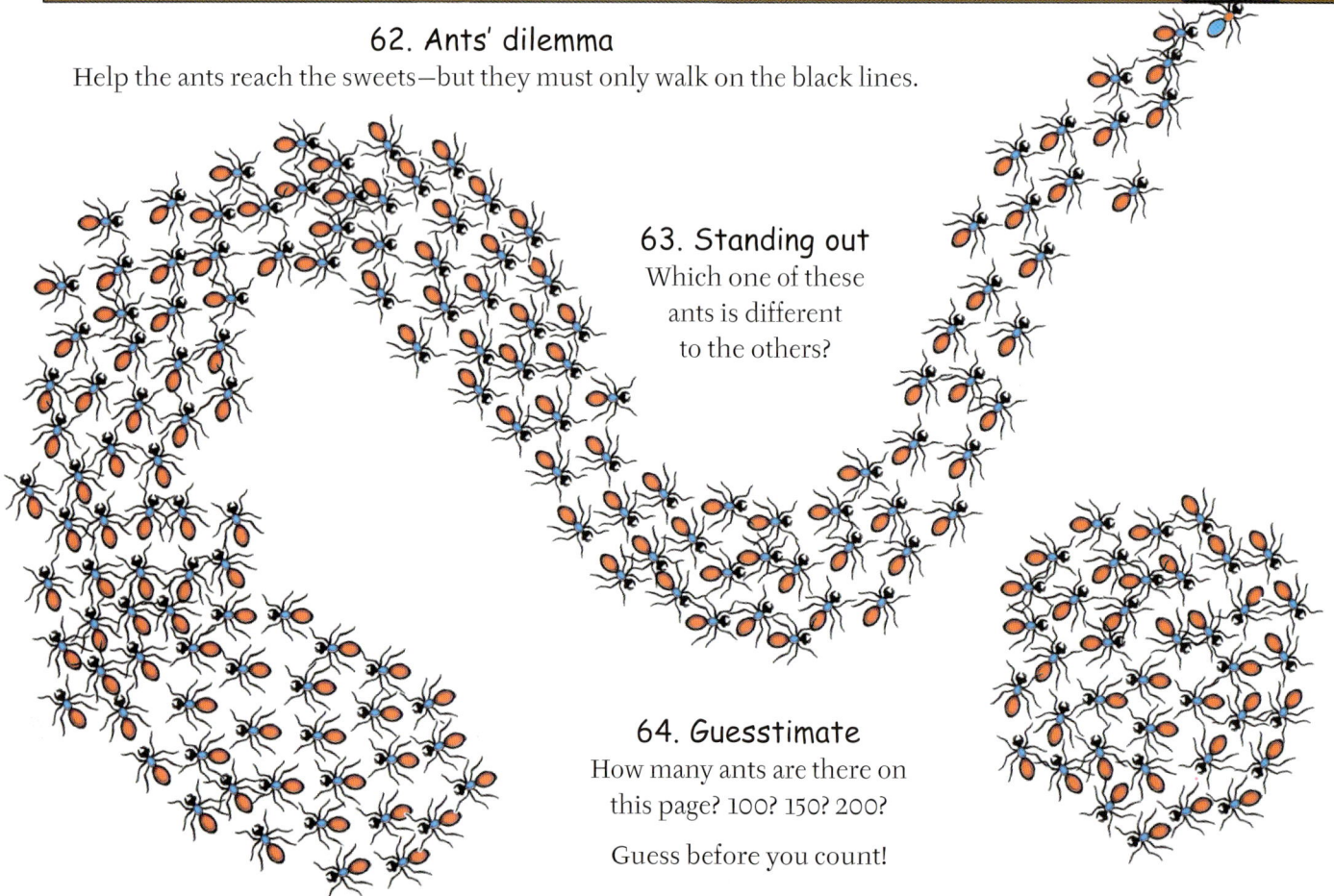

63. Standing out

Which one of these ants is different to the others?

64. Guesstimate

How many ants are there on this page? 100? 150? 200?

Guess before you count!

65. Little green pears Which of the four squares below should fill the blank space?

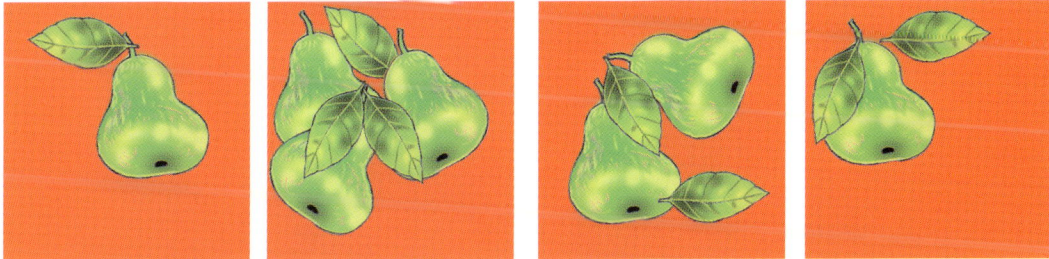

1.   2.   3.   4.

An apple equals half a pumpkin.

Four pears are worth one pumpkin.

Two lemons are worth two apples.

66. Value for money
Which of the six displays would cost the most?

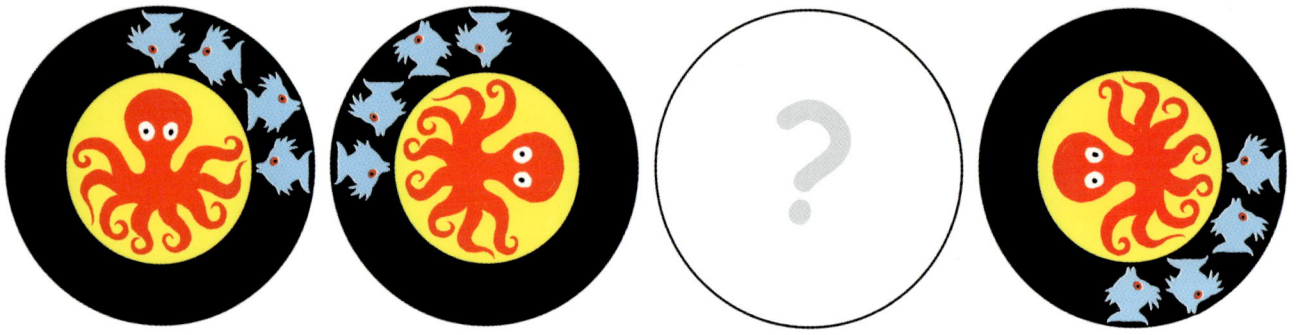

67. Octodiscs Which of the four circles below belongs in the empty space?

1. 2. 3. 4.

68. Danger!
Big-bellied silver cods are delicious—but those
with red eyes, green spots and forked tails are poisonous!

Are there any poisonous fish below?

69. Mutant amoeba
Do all of these amoebas look alike?

Check again—one is different.

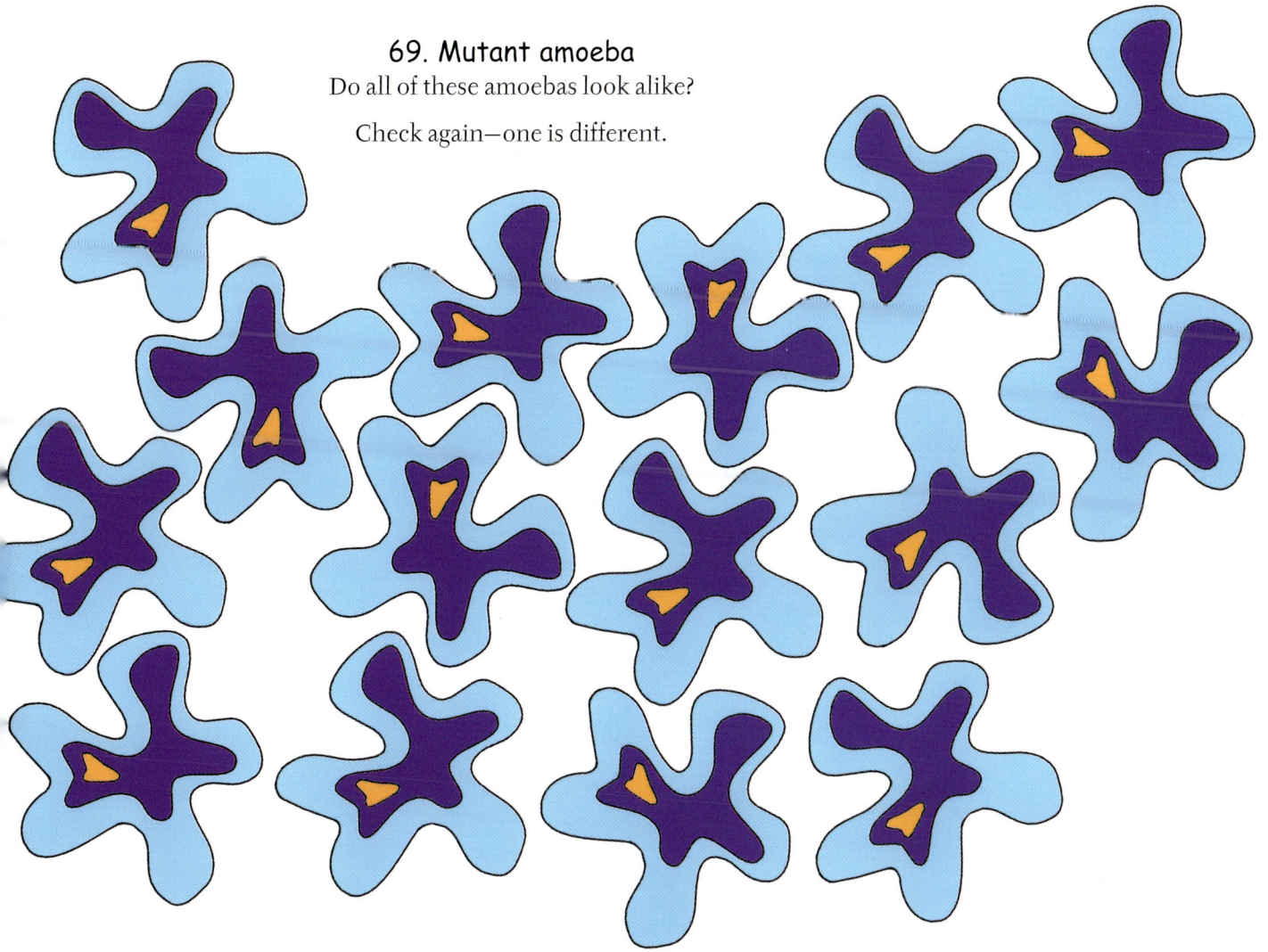

70. Untouchable bug
Which of these bugs is forever out of reach?

71. Look-alike pets

People and their pets often look alike!

Can you pick which animal belongs to whom?

72. Train your eyes
What number belongs
on the blue wagon?

Top row wagons: 2 5 2 9

Middle row: 8 1 3 4

Bottom row: 2 [blue wagon] 2 6

73. Follow that star!
Only one entrance will allow you
to reach the centre of the maze.

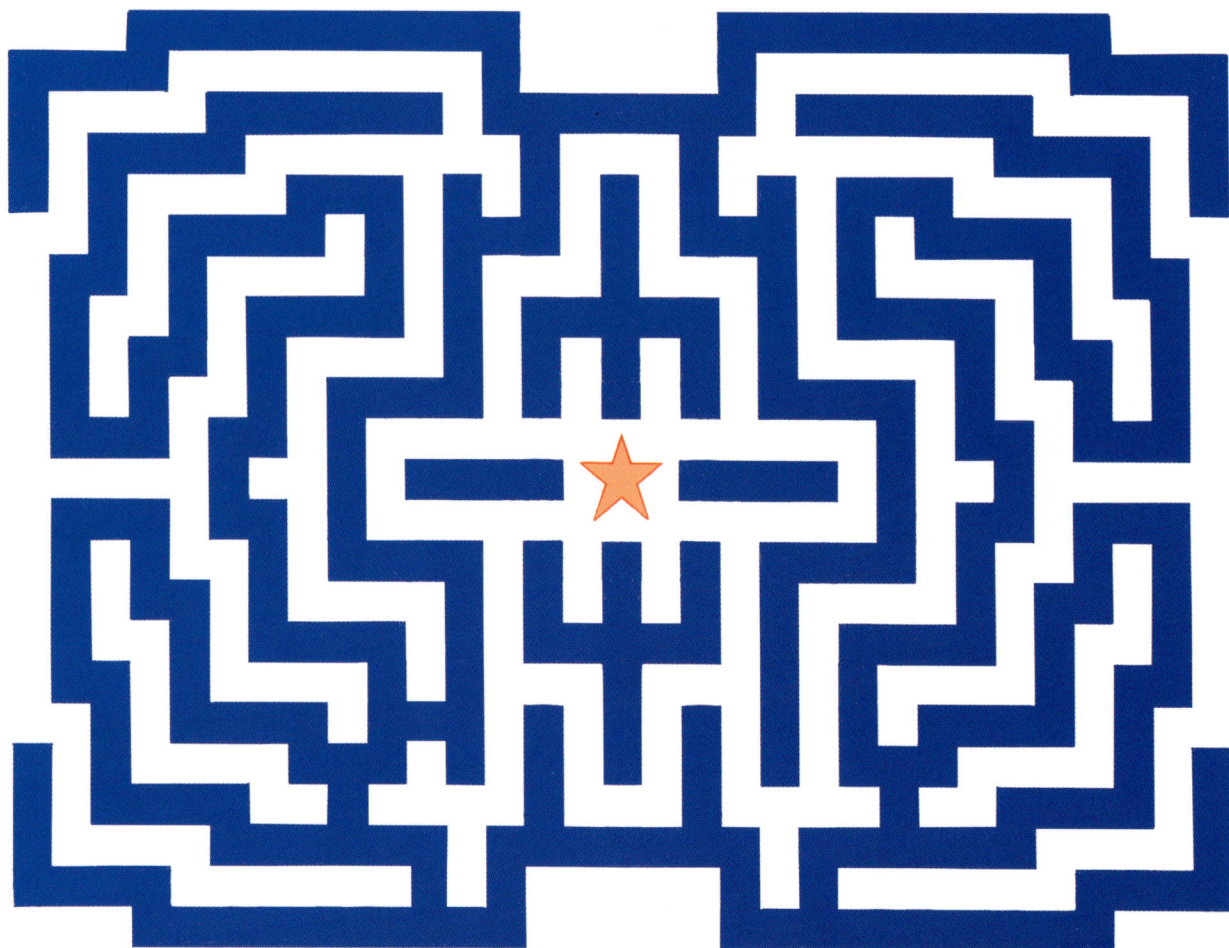

74. Three blanks
What numbers belong in the three blank octagons?

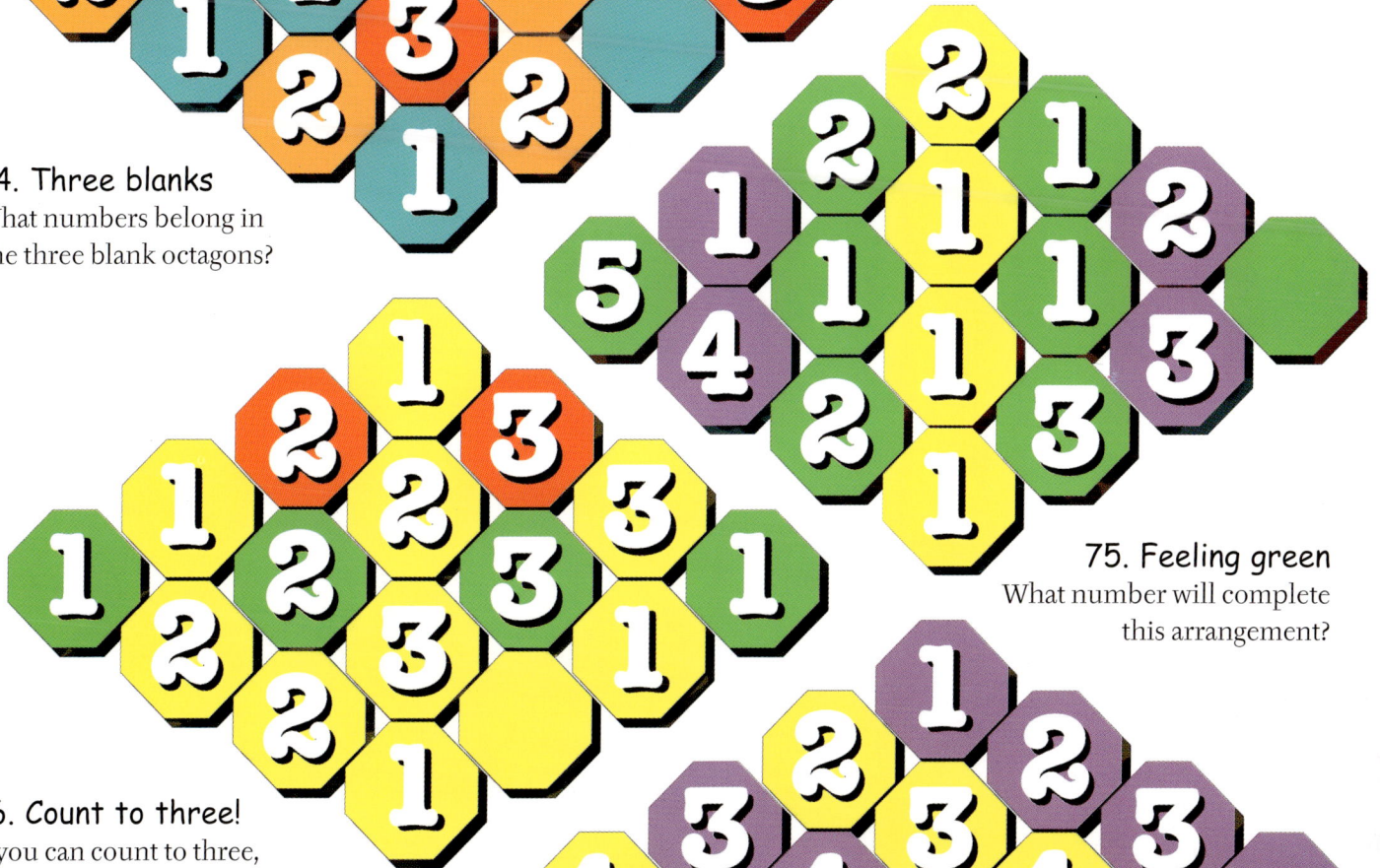

75. Feeling green
What number will complete this arrangement?

76. Count to three!
If you can count to three, you should be able to work out what the missing number is.

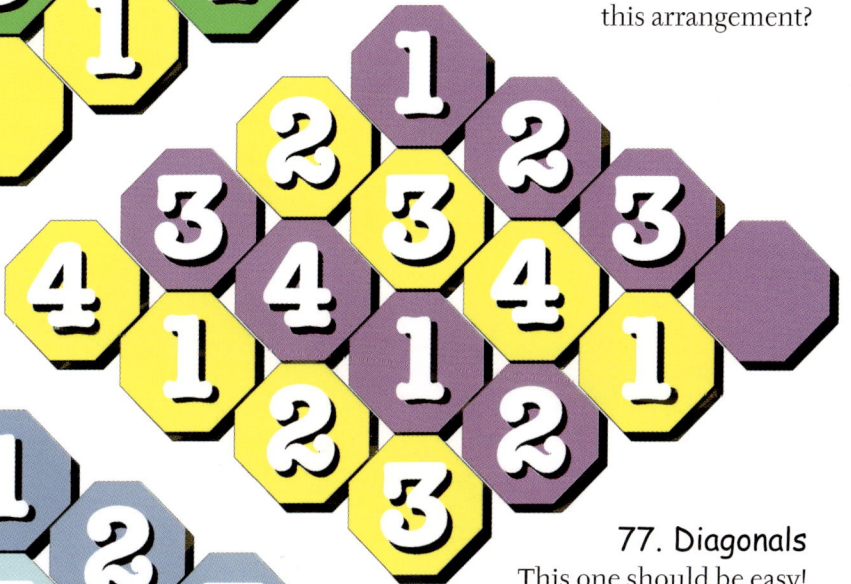

77. Diagonals
This one should be easy!

78. Code name: Spiral
And that's the clue for cracking this code...

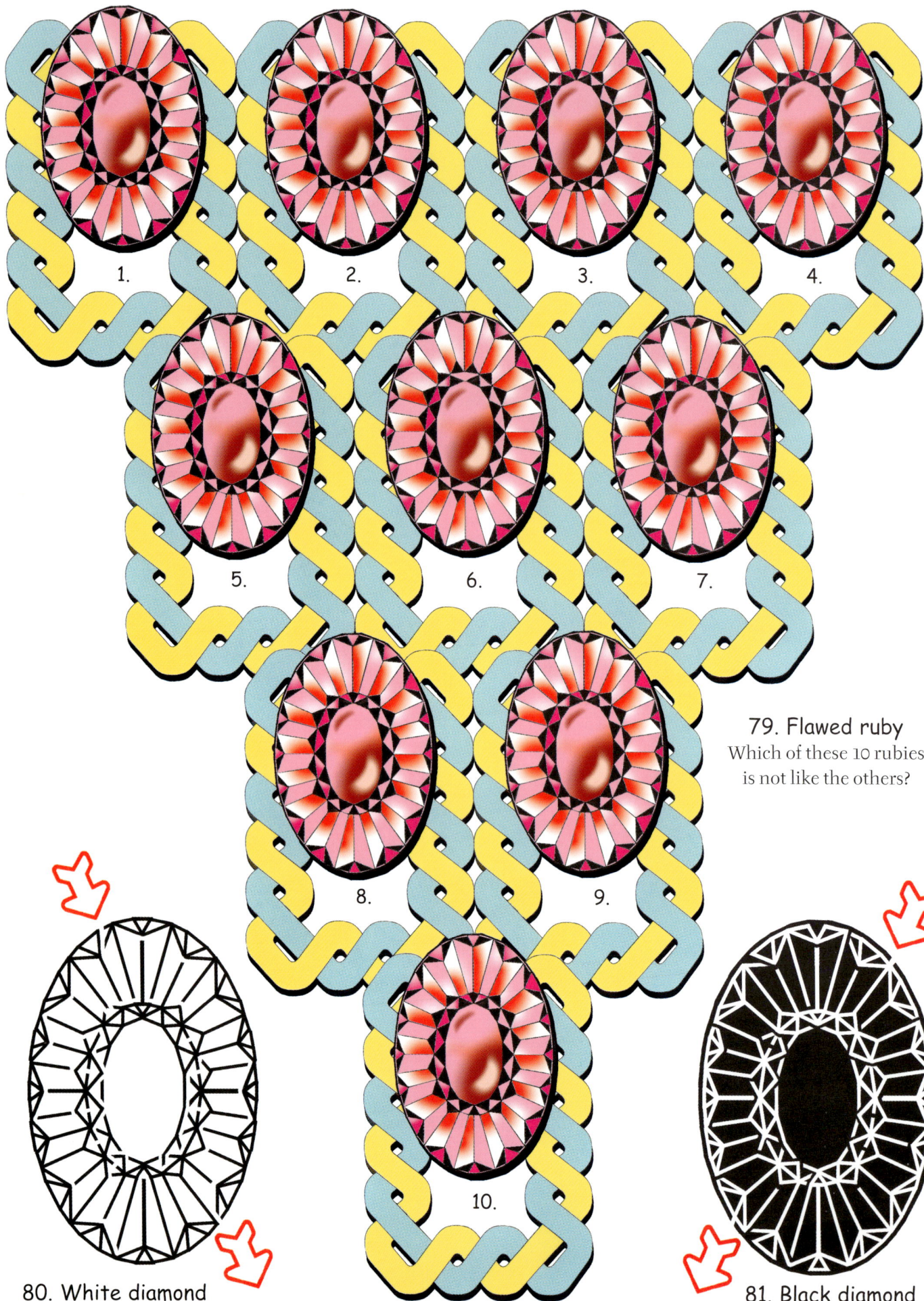

1.

2.

3.

4.

5.

6.

7.

79. Flawed ruby
Which of these 10 rubies
is not like the others?

8.

9.

80. White diamond

10.

81. Black diamond

82. Frogs and flowers Which of the six squares below belongs in the blank space?

1.

2.

3.

4.

5.

6.

83. Cubic error This is supposed to be the same cube drawn from four different angles—but one of these pictures is wrong.

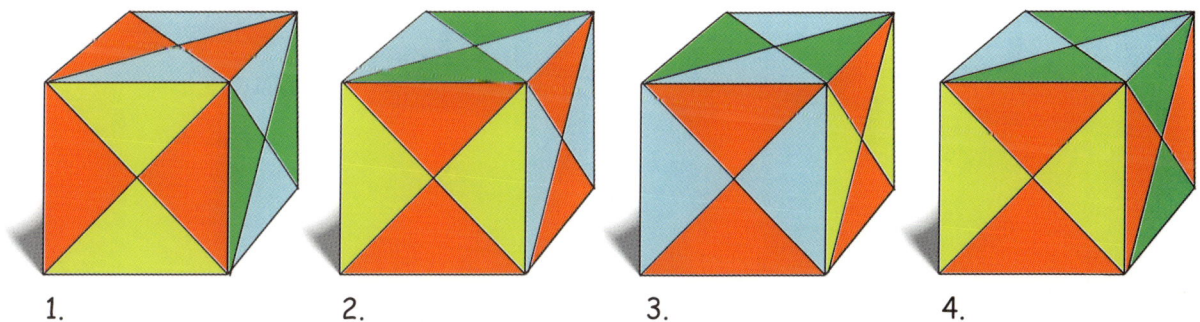

1.

2.

3.

4.

84. Frisky Frisbees

85. It's raining cats and dogs!
All the dogs seem identical,
but one is definitely different!

86. Catty conundrum
How many cats are different
(apart from their size)?

87. Clown beetles There are five varieties of clown beetles, but only four are represented in the collection above.

Can you spot the fifth variety?

88. Hidden face
Can you spot the face of this collector among the beetles?

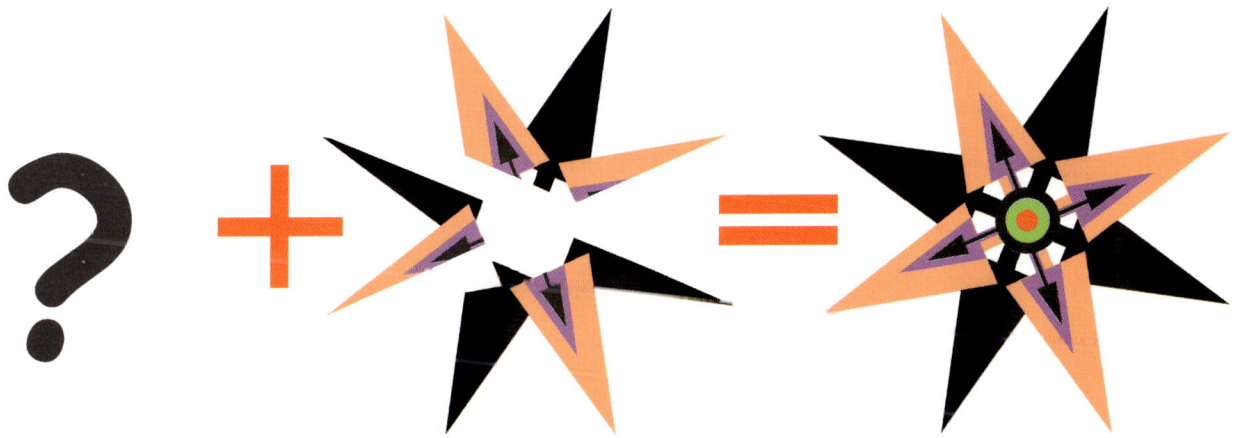

89. Star search
Which of the six fragments below will complete the star?

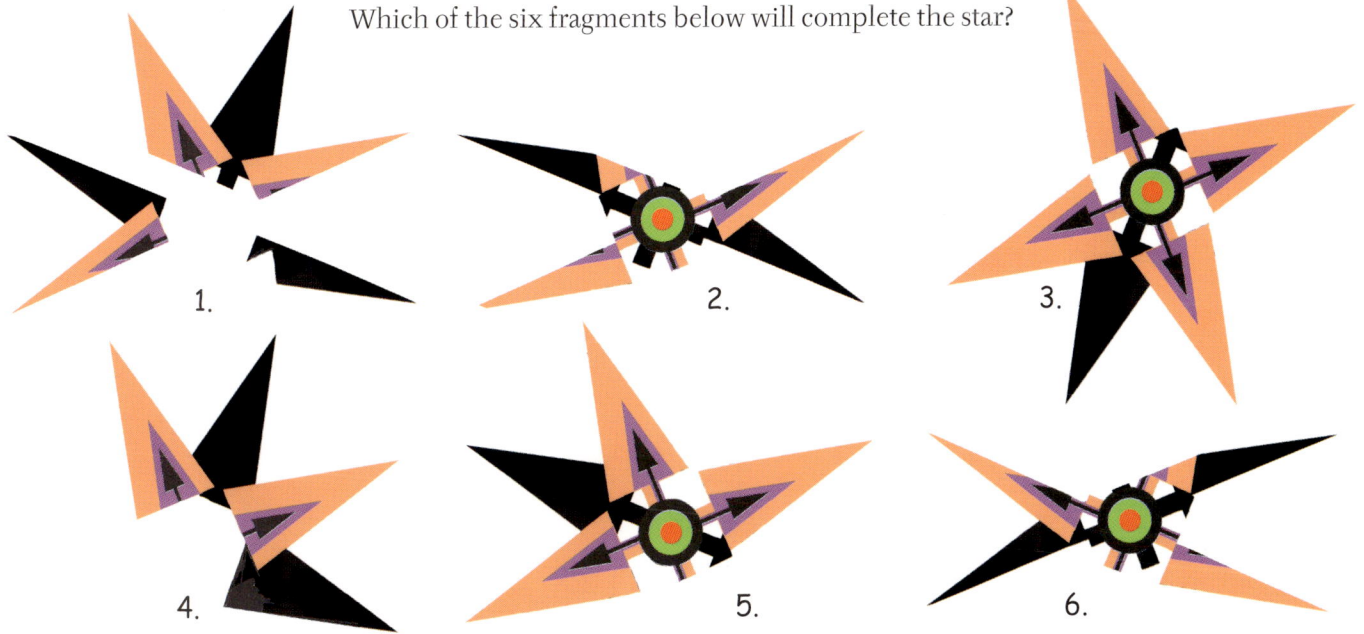

1.

2.

3.

4.

5.

6.

90. Bright brollies
All but one of the umbrellas have the same pattern.

Which is the odd one out?

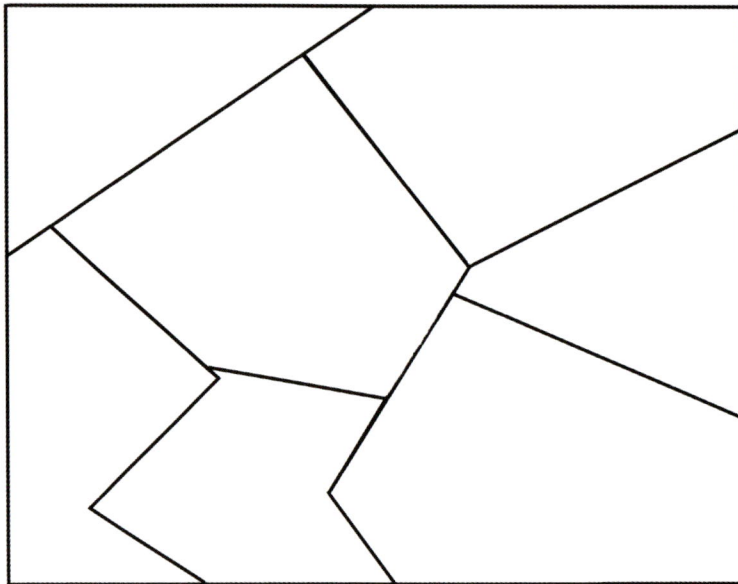

91. Shattered numbers

The house number on the above plate has been shattered.
Can you work out what the number was?

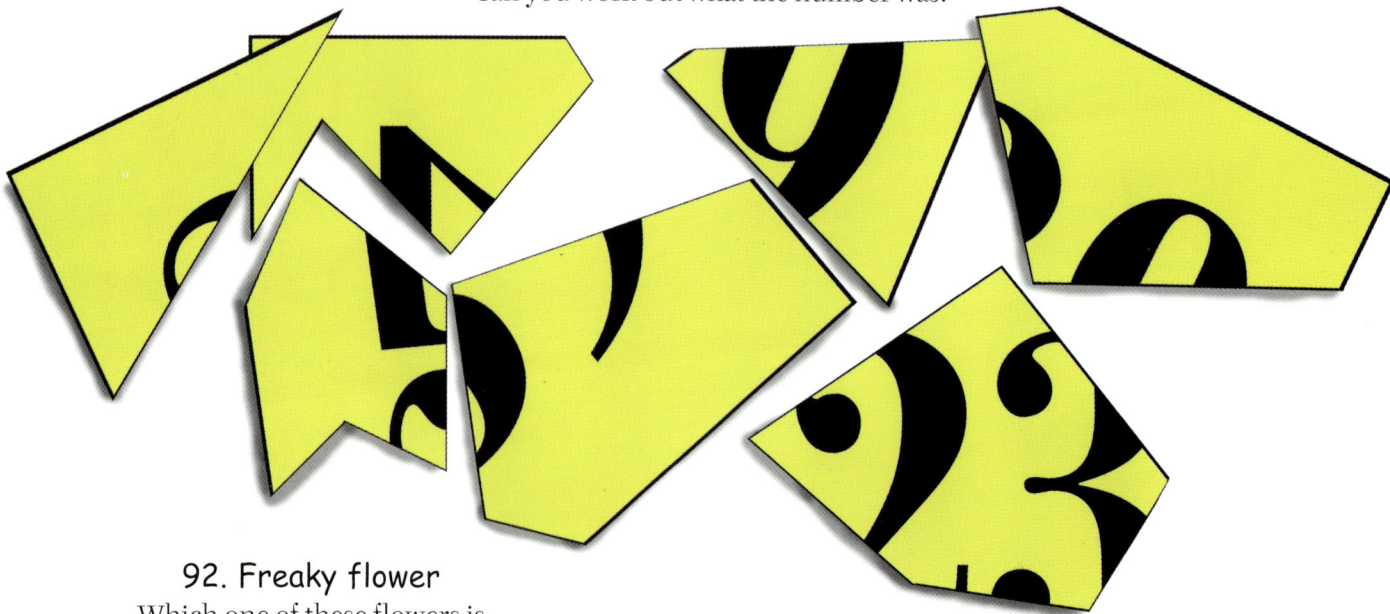

92. Freaky flower

Which one of these flowers is
botanically different to the others?

93. Stand-out sombreros
Three of these hats are different to the others.

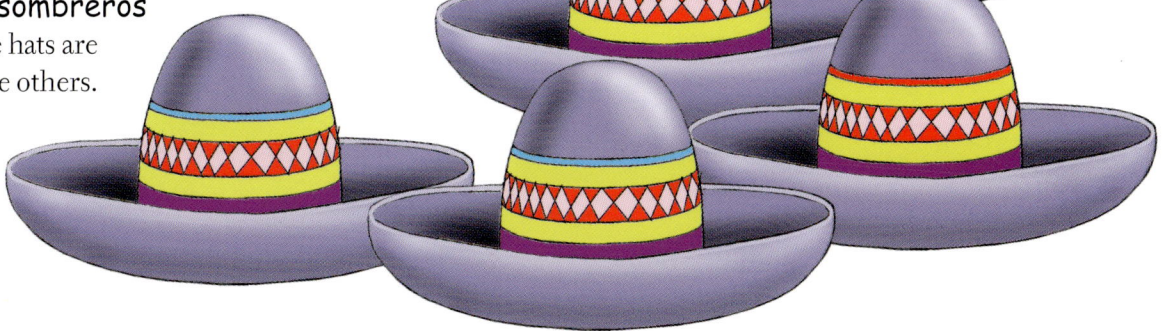

94. Wheels of fire Get through them as fast as you can!

95. Snake-necked catpeckers

Snake-necked catpeckers are playful birds, and not at all vicious.
It should only take a little prod with a stick to free poor Sooty.

But which bird must the farmer prod?

96. Shape search

Find these five hidden shapes!

Solutions

1. **Gift-giving** Both gifts have the same value.
2. **Fruit Platter** In order of value: 6 (31 pts), 2 (23 pts), 5 (22 pts), 1 (17 pts), 4 (8 pts), 3 (7 pts)
3. **Lost sock** The diplomat needs a Royal Mark.
4. **Star-crossed snake**
5. **Giant leaf** Number 2 is the only one who can reach the centre.
6. **Pillars of society** The topmost caterpillar has different spots.
7. **Apple turn-over** Each apple has turned 90° clockwise.
8. **Brush-rush** This maze is so easy you shouldn't even need a map!
9. **Double dragon trouble**
10. **Snail race** Diagram 4 is correct.
11. **Family reunion** The small snail on the bottom left with a yellow ribbon is the outsider—its shell spirals in a different direction.
12. **Three-in-a-row** The picture in the centre is left over.
13. **Odd one out** The pirate only has one leg—everything else has four.
14. **Copied keys** The yellow key wasn't copied.
15. **Apple snakes** The purple snake has eaten two red and two green apples.

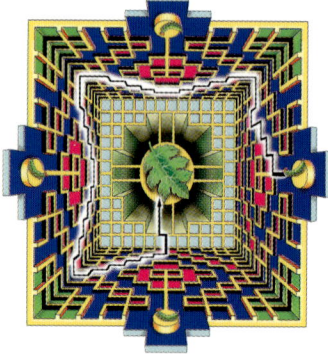

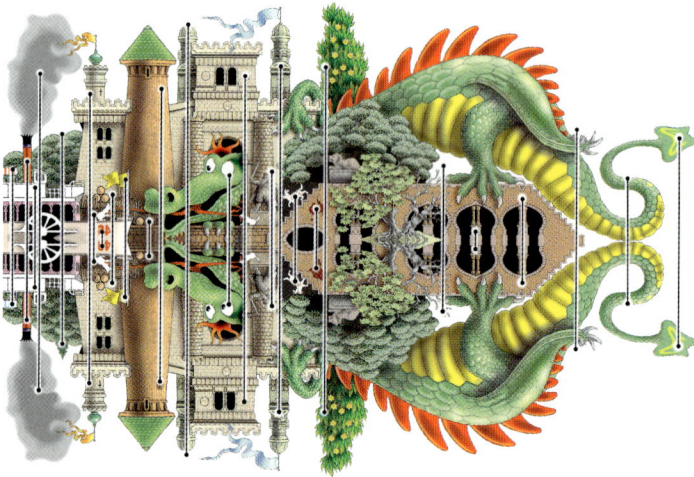

16. **Out of Reach**
17. **Butterfly friends** The two coloured butterflies are exactly the same. The red spots on the others indicate their differences.
18. **Pilot error** Check the wing tips of the lowest plane.
19. **Double-checking double-deckers** The bottom plane on the right has a flash that goes UNDER the red band.
20. **Day-dreamers** Use your imagination! Here are some: bear, fish, dog, kangaroo, sleeping cat, elephant, crocodile, lizard, bird.
21. **Fantastic faces** You should see at least 15.
22. **House cat** The first cat on the left lives at number 5—the cats' spots are the same colours as the curtains, and their tails are on the same side as the chimneys.
23. **Cat and mouse**
24. **Special delivery** The brown parcel goes to house number 10.
25. **Flower arrangement** The flowerbox goes to house number 6.
26. **Cat city!** There are 25 cats.
27. **Golden delicious**

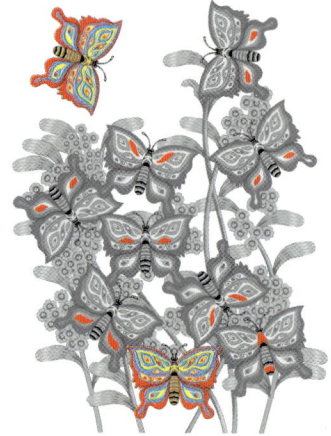

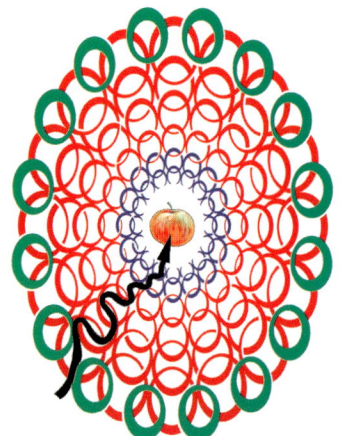

28. **Fractured star** Number 5 completes the star.

29. **Missing mandolin** Number 1 fits—the background colour alternates, while the number of strings increases by one each time.

30. **Missed a spot!** Number 4 belongs in the missing section.

31. **Through the butterfly**

32. **Apple-loving grub**

33. **Tree of life**
The arrows indicate the three spots.

34. **Starry, starry jungle**

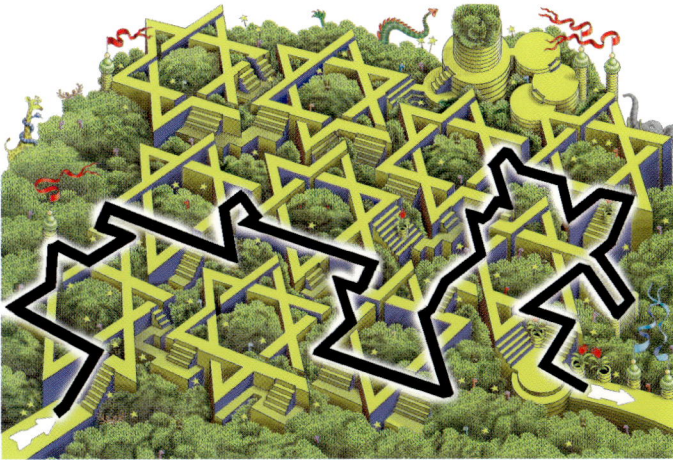

35. **Magic mandala**

36. **Odd one out** This is certainly not a heavenly body! All the others are...

37. **Colour code**

38. **Shady deals**

39. **Odd objects**

40. **All together now** The items in the big box add up to 59.

41. **Odd one out** It's the plane, of course! (It's not a musical instrument.)

42. **Vanishing violin case**

43. **Notable error** The last bar has an extra $\frac{1}{8}$ note.

44. **Spiders' nest** There are only 21 of these spiders, so they must be male.

There are 25 of these spiders, so they must be female.

45. **Coloured kites** The answer is number 7. (The colours of the tail always advance one place.)

46. **Giddy geckos** Most geckos have green hind feet, except those who will be able to find their way to the middle.

47. **Kite-flying competition** These two children didn't dress in the colours of their kites.

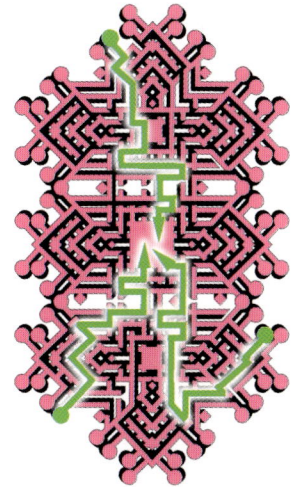

48. **Personal judgement** There's no right answer—it's just personal choice!

49. **Super balloons** Two blue balloons can lift 6 kg, and two green ones can lift 5. The total is 11 kg.

50. **Lift-off!** The total weight they can lift is 28 kg.

51. **Action Ant!**

52. **Teetering tower** Number 1 will balance the see-saw.

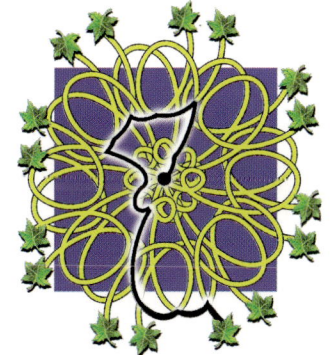

53. **Shaky balance** Number 1 will balance the see-saw.

54. **Tricky track**

55. **Pick a paddle** The paddles should add up to the number on her jumper.

56. **Short delivery** The door for number 8 is missing.

57. **Missing window** One of the windows for number 12 is missing.

58. **Trapped butterfly** The blue butterfly is trapped forever!

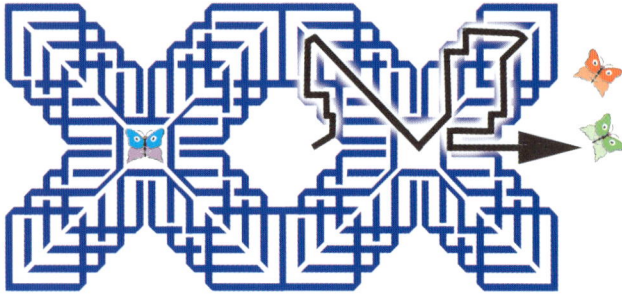

59. **Odd one out** The hand is the only object which is not symmetrical.

60. **Marsmathics** 2+2=4; 42+26=68; 84÷2=42

61. **Galactic superstore**

62. **Ants' dilemma**

63. **Standing out** The first ant has a blue body.

64. **Guesstimate** There are 186 ants in the picture.

65. **Little green pears** Number 2 is correct, with 3 pears and 3 leaves. (The number of pears in the top row increases by one, while the leaves decrease by one.)

66. **Value for money** The pears are clearly the cheapest. If we give each item a numerical value, pear=1; pumpkin=4; apple=2; lemon=2. So, square 1=15; 2=16; 3=6; 4=11; 5=21; 6=18. Square 5 is worth the most.

67. **Octodiscs** Disc number 4 is the best fit. Each octopus turns 90° clockwise, while the outer rim turns 90° counter-clockwise.

68. **Danger!** There is one poisonous fish!

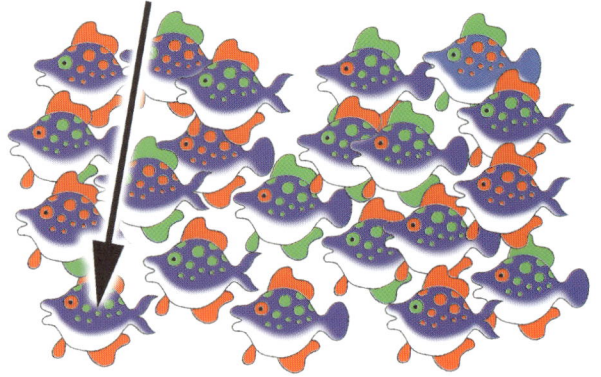

69. **Mutant amoeba** This is the only different one.

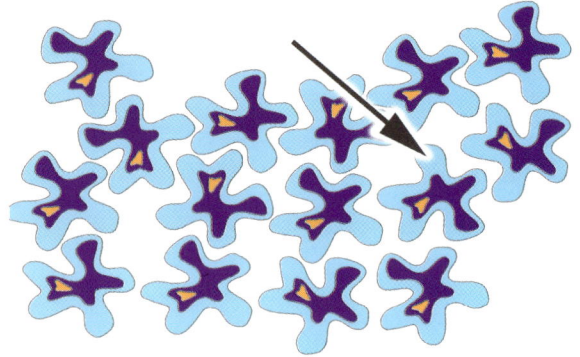

70. **Untouchable bug** The green-and-red bug can't be reached.

71. **Look-alike pets** Follow the black lines.

72. **Train your eyes** The number 2 belongs on the blue wagon. (The wagons add up to the number in the locomotive.)

73. **Follow that star!**

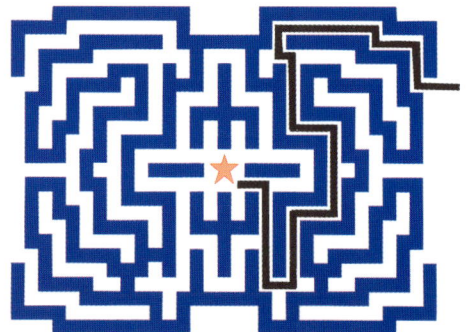

74. **Three blanks** Blue octagons are 1, red octagons are 3, orange octagons are 2.

75. *Feeling green* Each vertical column adds up to 5.

76. **Count to three!** Reading horizontally, the numbers 1, 2 and 3 are repeated. The blank space needs a 3.

77. **Diagonals** All the diagonals add up to 10, so the blank space needs a 4.

78. **Code name: Spiral** If you start from the left side and go clockwise, the numbers 1, 2, 3 and 4 are repeated in a spiral. The blank space needs a 4.

79. **Flawed ruby** Number 6 is different.

80. White diamond   81. Black diamond

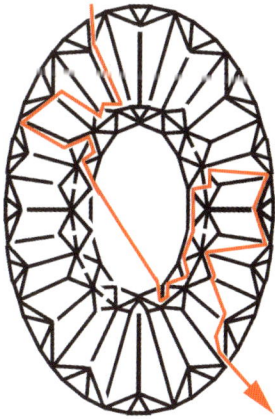

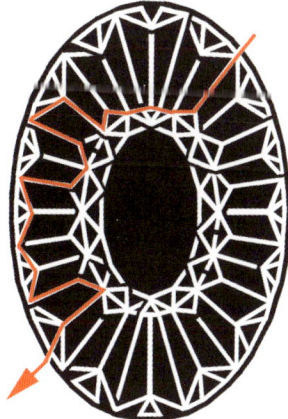

82. **Frogs and flowers** Number 1 belongs in the blank space. The inner row of red squares turns 90° counter-clockwise, while the outer row turns 90° clockwise.

83. **Cubic error** Number 4 is wrong. (Opposite sides are always the same.)

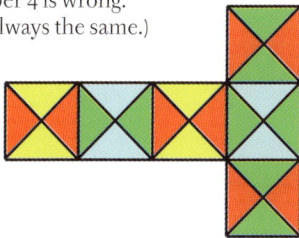

84. Frisky frisbees

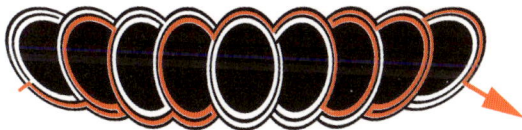

85. It's raining cats and dogs! and
86. **Catty conundrum** Three cats are different to the others.

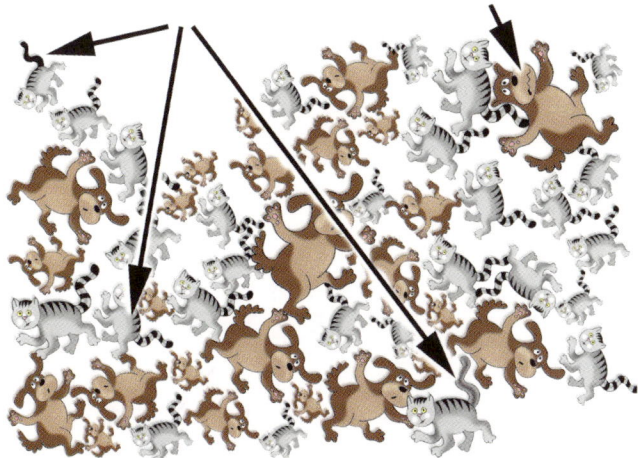

87. **Clown beetles** and
88. **Hidden face** The coloured beetle is the fifth variety. The white area marks the face.

89. **Star search** Number 2 completes the star.

90. **Bright brollies** The umbrella in the top left corner is different.

91. Shattered numbers

92. **Freaky flower** This flower has six petals instead of five.

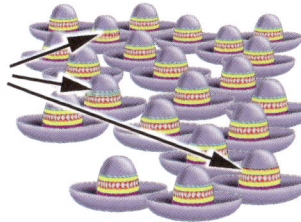

93. **Stand-out sombreros** These hats are different.

94. Wheels of fire

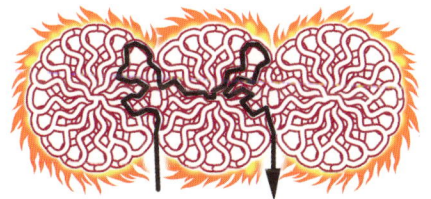

95. Snake-necked catpeckers and
96. Shape search

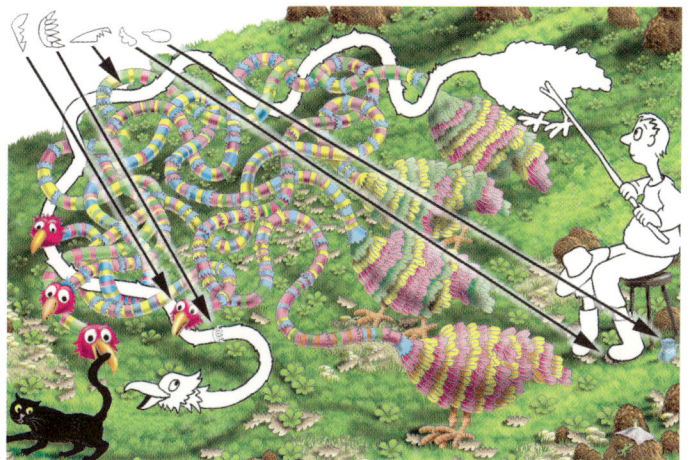

Rolf Heimann was born in Dresden, Germany in 1940. In 1945, he witnessed the total destruction of his home city — which made him a lifelong pacifist.

At age 18 he migrated to Australia. Over the next few years he worked his way around the country doing all kinds of jobs, including fruit-picking, labouring at railways and working in factories. Every spare hour was spent writing and sketching.

Eventually, he settled in Melbourne, where he worked for printers and publishers before finally running his own art studio.

In 1974, he sailed his own boat around the Pacific (and met his future wife, Lila, in Samoa), returning to Australia after two years to concentrate on painting, writing, cartooning and illustrating.

He has now published over twenty books of puzzles and mazes. His books have travelled to dozens of countries, and have sold millions of copies around the world.

Also by Rolf Heimann from Little Hare Books
AstroMaze
Zoodiac

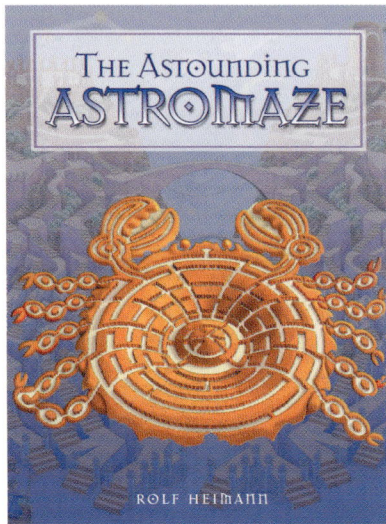
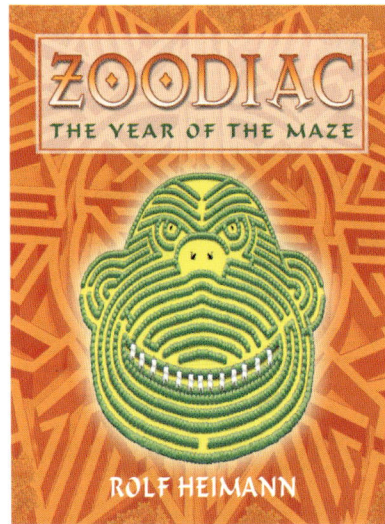